6X

The Uncensored Confessions

Part One

NINA MALKIN

Hodder
Children's
Books

a division of Hodder Headline Limited

Text copyright © 2005 Nina Malkin

First published in the USA in 2005
by Scholastic Inc.

This edition published in 2006
by Hodder Children's Books

The right of Nina Malkin to be identified as the Author of
this Work has been asserted by her in accordance with the
Copyright, Designs and Patents Act 1988.

A Catalogue record for this book is available from the British Library

ISBN 0 340 91150 6

Typeset in Bembo by Avon DataSet Ltd,
Bidford on Avon, Warwickshire

Printed and bound in Great Britain by
Bookmarque Ltd, Croydon, Surrey

The paper and board used in this paperback are natural recyclable
products made from wood grown in sustainable forests.
The manufacturing processes conform to the environmental
regulations of the country of origin.

Hodder Children's Books
a division of Hodder Headline Ltd
338 Euston Road
London NW1 3BH

PART ONE
INTRODUCING 6X

'You got some dirty boots, baby . . .'

— *Sonic Youth, 'Dirty Boots'*

'When you're around, I'm somebody else . . .'

— *Guided by Voices, 'Teenage FBI'*

'You can rock me just about anywhere . . .'

— *The Cars, 'You're All I've Got Tonight'*

'The waiting is the hardest part . . .'

— *Tom Petty, 'The Waiting'*

The Body

They call me The Body, though not to my face. Not that I would care. Maybe I would, I don't know. Technically, I know I have a good body. I'm five-ten, wear size ten jeans, and my boobs are a double-D. My mother says I should be proud of my body; she certainly is. I'm sorry, does that sound terrible? It's just that I read in a magazine about a girl my age who had a boob reduction – I mentioned that to my mom and she looked at me like I'd asked to be decapitated. Plus she's forever ordering me to stand up straight and put my shoulders back – a drill sergeant in socialite's clothing. When I started to develop, she would brag to her friends. Not that she actually takes credit for my body; in fact, she's always saying things like 'It must be something in the water!' But that's how she thinks of me – as her creation.

Or her project. Because before 6X was anything, when it was just a crazy, this-will-never-happen-in-a-million-years idea, my mom was all for it. Not me. Even now, with our video on MTV ninety-seven times a day, it hasn't fully sunk in, since the way it started out was so unreal, so stupid. A big fat joke – with me as the punch line. But like it or not, here I am in front of a camera,

1

spilling all. Uch, I'm sorry, it's just so completely embarrassing – I made *such* a fool of myself.

It was the holidays, and my stepdad's law firm was having a party at the Drake House, very fancy, all the lawyers and all the big clients. There was no reason for me to go – there wouldn't be any people my age, no kids to talk to – but my mother was like, 'You're going.' Any excuse to get me out of jeans and into a dress by whatever designer currently has her in thrall.

So I went (you do not argue with my mother), and I swear, there is nothing more mind-numbing than watching a ballroom full of old people party. Waiters trudged around with trays of champagne and I thought: *Why not?* Nobody blinked when I took a glass. So I took another. I wasn't drinking to get drunk, though. It's more that I was bored and uncomfortable – holding a glass gave me something to do.

Sipping and walking, sipping and walking – that was my evening. Until all that sipping made walking kind of a challenge. I went to stand by the edge of the stage and watch the band, even though they were Top 40 – definitely not my thing. Soon as they took a break, the drummer came up to hit on me, which was *so* not appropriate. I mean, I'm a guest, and I'm fifteen. Anyway, I didn't know what to say – I'm pretty shy in general, and I get extra shy around guys who consider my boobs tantamount to the aurora borealis. But there I am – hello, little drunk girl – telling him how cool I thought it was that he played drums, because *I* always wanted to play drums – which wasn't true, I'd never even thought about it.

Next thing I know, he's leading me onto the stage and sitting me behind the kit and telling me what to do. I just start banging away, but within minutes my mom's unacceptable behaviour radar picks up on my unacceptable behaviour, and she dispatches my stepdad. Only he's not alone; he's with one of his partners, Brian Wandweilder – this entertainment lawyer, a real hotshot, the youngest partner at the firm.

'Well, well, well, Sherman,' Mr Wandweilder said to my stepdad. 'I didn't know Wynnie played drums.'

My stepdad smirked at him. 'She doesn't,' he said, then gave the drummer a dirty look and took my arm to help me down. I didn't complain; I was too busy babbling, 'That was so much fun! Oh my God, that was SO FUN!' Such a ditz, I know – but the weird thing was Mr Wandweilder kept going on about how incredible I was. Under normal circumstances – in other words, not drunk ones – I would have been mortified, but we talked about me playing the drums for a long time. There was something just so earnest about him: pale brown eyes behind little wire-rimmed glasses, sandy hair, not *long* long but not lawyer short – sort of flopping as he nodded with an enthusiasm, an excitement, that was more kidlike than adult. Mr Wandweilder talking about me and music and the drums made my stupid drunk girl act seem not just acceptable but, I don't know, credible . . . cool.

And later that night, in the limo coming home, my mom and stepdad were discussing it.

My stepdad was like: 'And if you can believe it, Cynthia, Wandweilder actually said he could put a band together around Wynnie and sell it.'

'Why wouldn't I believe it?' my mom said. She had that out-of-breath sound in her voice that she gets when she's irritated.

3

'Wynn is a poised, beautiful, talented girl. And simply because Brian's never developed a band before . . . he knows the industry. You always say that. Do you think he was joking?'

'No, I actually think he *was* serious,' my stepdad said, loosening his tie. 'But he doesn't know Wynn. Really, Cynthia – can you envision our Wynnie bopping around onstage, playing drums in a rock band?'

They're having this conversation with me sitting between them in the limo. They're talking about me, and I'm sitting right there. And it's not like I'm passed out and drooling; I'm just a little drowsy.

'You're not denying that my daughter is poised and beautiful and talented, are you?' my mother said, raising an eyebrow in warning.

'Of course not,' he replied quickly. 'But Wynnie? In a band? Playing drums? Don't you think that's slightly ridiculous?'

My mom patted my stepdad's hand and called him darling. 'What *isn't* ridiculous?' she said. 'One of the Harton hotel girls married a midget – an actual midget! Arnold Schwarzenegger was elected governor of California. We live in the age of ridiculous.' She looked at me and smoothed my hair and smiled. 'I'm not even thinking about Wynn actually being *good* at it, of her having any kind of success. I simply think it might bring her out of her shell.'

'Maybe,' said my stepdad. He was quiet for a minute, mulling it over – he's like that, always looks at all the angles. 'Maybe,' he said again. Then it was his turn to look at me and smooth my hair and smile. 'I just hope she doesn't come out of her *shirt*.'

The Voice

They call me The Voice. Oh gosh, no – not officially! That would be so rude. Because it's not like the other kids aren't talented. Because they are. Really. Just sometimes at Universe, our record label, they will say that. It's kind of a slang thing in the industry to say 'she's the voice' instead of 'she's the lead singer.' Anyway, singing is what I do. Always has been.

Ask anyone in my family and they'll tell you about 'The Nudge.' We were all there in church – my mom and daddy, my grandparents, basically the whole town of Frog Level, South Carolina. And when the singing started, I opened my mouth like everyone else … and out it came. My voice. My mom says it was the sweetest, truest sound she ever heard – like an angel – but she had no idea it was little old me.

Well, once she realized it was *my* voice, she stopped singing herself and nudged my daddy with her elbow. He couldn't believe it either, so he nudged my granddad, next to him in the pew. And then it was like the wave – you know, the wave they do at football games? Like that. The Nudge started moving through the congregation until every last person, except for the preacher, got The Nudge and stopped singing and it was just me, three and a half years old, belting out *What a Friend We Have in Jesus* like nobody's business. It was my first solo.

Gosh, that's a back-home story for you. All my family is still down there in Frog Level. That old church isn't there any more but I can remember it: white clapboard, wooden floor, and so tiny — standing room only on any given Sunday. Isn't memory strange? I think it is. Because even though I can remember that church, what I cannot remember, what I wish I *could* remember more than anything, is my daddy. I cannot see his smile, his eyes, his hands, his hair; I cannot see any part of him anywhere in my mind.

What happened was, he got killed defending our country in the Gulf War. And my mom doesn't have any pictures of him — they went missing because my mom and I moved around so much. It took us a while to get all the way up to New York — well, New Jersey; right now we live in Elizabeth, New Jersey. What happened was, after we lost my daddy, my mom had to work real hard at the Wal-Mart and go to college, but once she earned her degree she kept on looking for better and better jobs. We'd stay in a place for a bit, but if she didn't get promoted, well, then it was 'who can do better?' And for some reason the better the job, the farther up North it was. She's got a wonderful position now; they love her. My mom is serious about her career; she is an *executive* at the top of middle management. As supportive as she is about me being a star and all, she would never up and quit her job. It's *hers*. It's one of the things that makes me so proud of her.

Gosh, I could go on and on about my mom — but I'm supposed to be talking about me. Well, 'round about the time we moved here, I dropped my first name, LuAnn, and started going by Kendall, which is my middle name. I was entering all these pageants and talent shows, and it just sounded so much more sophisticated and professional: Kendall Taylor. Only when I go back home to visit, I go by LuAnn – my mom says so. LuAnn is my great grandmomma's name, so it's out of respect. Me going by Kendall, nobody down there even knows about that; my mom says it's our secret. Although, gosh, with all that's going on now – I mean, we're on MTV! – pretty soon the folks in Frog Level will catch wind, and I can't imagine what my mom will tell them all.

Anyway, all those pictures of my daddy. Lost. It's sad, I think, but I don't dwell on it, because I am a very positive person. Plus I know my daddy's up on a cloud, watching all the awesome things that are happening for me. Sometimes I like to think that when I sing, my daddy is starting a Nudge right there in heaven!

The Boss

Call me a bitch and you better watch your back. Just kidding! Look, no offence but it's dumb to try to label the members of this band. Back in the boy-band era maybe that's what they did – he's the poet, he's the bad boy, he's the sex god – but please, that is over. It's just stereotyping, which I am personally very much against, and which our band is so not about. Because check it out, here's the black girl and she's not in an R&B group and she's not even the singer. Our band is about breaking barriers.

But whatever, if these video diaries get turned into a reality show or some kind of special-bonus-extra content for our CD, and that helps sell records – cool. See, that's how my mind works. I am a businesswoman. First and foremost. And an artist. An artist and a businesswoman. Besides, it's not like I have a problem big-upping myself, and venting is good because I get to have my say. I mean, let's be real: when 6X does press – for a magazine, or a talk show, any of that shit – I'm always gonna get left out. For two very, um, *obvious* reasons, everyone wants to talk to Barbie – oops, I mean Wynn, but it's OK, keep that in; she knows I call her Barbie. And then they wanna talk to

Kendall, since she's the singer – fine. And then they wanna talk to A/B, because he's the only boy and they wanna know what that's like; plus he's a cutie in that 'Hot? Who? *Moi!?*' kind of way and all our chick fans wanna hear from him. So by the time the interview is over, oops, they run out of tape and time and nobody gets a chance to ask me a single thing. Which is retarded, because I'm the only one in the band that's got anything to say. I have a *vocabulary,* all right. Do I have to show you my standardized test scores?

Look, I don't mean to be harsh. It's not like I'm in a band with a bunch of morons. A/B is really smart, and he's funny as shit, but he's an eat-sleep-breathe-fill-in-whatever-bodily-function-you-want kind of music junkie. And Kendall's smart in that bouncy, chirpy, goody-two-shoes way. On the low, every now and then Kendall will come out with something whack, but mostly she works the little angel thing, which means she is pure vanilla without the bean. Then Wynn, well, between you and me and the whole entire world, I'm not sure what it is with her because I think – I *know* – my girl's got some pretty deep thoughts going on behind that wispy honey-coloured fringe, but her favourite two sentences are 'I'm sorry' and 'I don't know.'

Not me. I've got opinions. I've got ideas. I make shit happen. Like that day in school, when Wynn first brought up the band thing in homeroom. We both go to Little Red Schoolhouse. Yes, that is really the name of our school – so cute I could vomit. Personally, I think my parents could spend their hard-earned money on other things than private school for me – and I could definitely live without taking two trains into Manhattan from Brooklyn every day. But my dad teaches maths at a junior high that's so ghetto, the kids call it Jay-Z J.H.S. The shit he's witnessed on the job, you know he'd rather sleep on tacks then send me to state school. As to my mom, she believes overpaying for my education will keep me from turning out like my half brother John Joseph, aka JJ, aka Loserboy. He's the fruit of her first marriage to one of the goombah guys from her old neighbourhood, before she went all jungle fever and got with my dad.

Only forget my family – you wanna hear about 6X. Back in the day, Wynn wasn't exactly a friend, but we had a few classes together, we talked. Well, one time she's telling me about some chichi champagne-fuelled night out, and this drummer dude who's clearly trying to find a way into her thong. I'm half-listening to this shit, but the second she gets to the part about her stepdad's law partner claiming he could build a band around her, I snap to. I mean, I'm riveted. Right away, I'm like: 'Really? I play bass.'

And that weekend, I learned how.

That's where Loserboy came in. Twenty-five years old, can't even hold a job at the freakin' post office . . . pathetic. My dad does his best to ignore JJ – which is tough, seeing as how he's been living in our basement since his own father kicked him out – but I love him like crazy, he's my big brother, all right. So he's got this bass (he was in a band for five minutes once), and that Friday night we put on the Ramones' *Leave Home* and *Rocket to Russia* – old-school punk is one of the few things me and JJ have in common – and I strap on his big-ass Fender P. It comes down below my knees and looks retarded, but he teaches me a couple of bass lines and all weekend I practise. The next Monday at school I'm all over Wynn about the band, the band, the band.

And if that makes me pushy or aggressive or a bitch then, fine, whatever . . .

The Boy

Ah yes: The Boy. The dude, the guy, the Y chromosome. That would be me. Most of all, though, I'm the musician. Every band's gotta have at least one. Not to be a complete asshole but hey, we've all got our jobs.

Wynn's job is to be the babe. Oh, she keeps the beat OK – believe me, when I first heard her, man, I was like 'no way,' but it's amazing how much she's improved. Only come on, calling her 'attractive' is like saying the Grand Canyon is a hole in the ground, and I don't just mean her body, it's the details – her heart-shaped face and those eyes, not quite green, not quite blue. Even her earlobes are hot, her clavicle. She could be up there hitting a bucket with a pair of knitting needles and people would still shell out twenty bucks to watch her. As to the other half of our rhythm section, Stella, she's also a graduate of the leaps-and-bounds improvement programme. Still, playing bass is not her main thing. Hmm, how can I put this? Stella's job is to be the boss. We've got a manager and an A&R guy and a lawyer and a label, but Stella's the boss because she scares the crap out of us. The girl was a Mafia kingpin or a Third World dictator in a former life, I shit you not.

Kendall, obviously, her job is to sing. She's one of those people, you hand them the phone book and when they start singing it, your jaw drops, you get goose bumps, the whole nine. So you could say that Kendall's a musician, too, but I beg to differ. She's something else: a natural. Never took a lesson. Pure gift. Me, I got some gift action going – at the risk of coming off completely obnoxious, I *can* play anything – but while Kendall just does it, I have to work at it. You can't hand me the didgeri-doo or the tuba and bang-zoom, prodigious brilliance. You got to give me a couple of days alone with it. Not like I've got much else to do, since I don't have a girlfriend efficiently running my life at the moment. Hey, I'm not Bo-Bo the Dog-Faced Boy, but at my school if you haven't stepped right out of an Abdominals and Fitch ad – if your hair's a little shaggy or your muscles don't have muscles – you're deemed wholly undroolworthy by the girl-powers-that-be.

Anyhoo, like I said, I have to work at music, only it's not work, because I love it.

And the point is, it doesn't matter to me if 6X is chicks or Chihuahuas, I'm just happy to be part of a band that's going somewhere. I'm seventeen years old, and I've been in eight different bands, so the fact that we're signed with a hit single out and ready to make our record is, to me, *finally*. Not just 'all right!' but also 'all right, *already*.' Even my mom and dad are resolving their considerable conflicts about my career choice now. Typical Jewish parents: you slide out of the womb and they practically slap you onto the piano seat, but God forbid you actually want to *do* music instead of be a doctor or a lawyer or a nuclear physicist, and it's as if you handed them massive two-for-one heart attacks. I don't care – I'll always do music. Say I become the CEO of some enormous bloodsucking conglomerate one day, I'll still do music on the side, and if I got a record deal, I'd call a board meeting and be like, 'Later, dudes . . .'

I was eleven in my first band, a cover band, classic rock. Everyone else was in their late twenties and thirties. I was the gimmick, the little piano prodigy. We'd play bars all over Long Island; my mother was not into it, but my dad convinced her it was OK because his kid brother was in the band. Uncle Dick. And his first name is not Richard, he's just an asshole. We'd do all the alphabet bands – BTO, ELO, ELP, and of course those quintessential and still-going-strong monsters of rock, AC/DC. Miraculously, the experience didn't turn me off to music. In fact, I loved it – I still get the warm-and-fuzzies when I hear AC/DC or the Floyd.

Still, by age thirteen I'd switched to guitar as my main instrument and started a band with some kids on my block. Here's the rest of my musical résumé to date: I had a ska-punk band; an emo band; a very strange duo with this guy from camp – me on guitar and keyboards and him on oboe and flute; your basic generic rock band; a very short-lived nu-metal thing; and two things I can only categorize with the meaningless tag of 'indie rock.' Where did they all go? Nowhere. Guys would move away, or get into sports or girls or drugs too much; or we would just disintegrate for some other reason.

So about a year or so ago, while trying to disentangle myself from the last indie-rock thing without making anybody hate me, I started doing the coffeehouse open-mike circuit. Just me and my six-string soul mate, Dan Electro, taking the Long Island Railroad into Manhattan, plugging in between all these whiny-sensitive acoustic-guitar guys, doing a set of obscure covers and crappy originals (a master songsmith I am not). Yet somehow that's how I hooked up with a manager, who turned out to be a major dickwad, but through him I met this guy who knew a lawyer who hooked me up with the girls, and now we're 6X, pop-rock sensation, superstars in training.

Does that sound simple as A-B-C? One-two-three? Vini, vidi, vici? Yeah, right . . .

The Body

Before our leap – OK, stumble – onto the rock scene came a little lull called Christmas vacation. My mom and stepdad took me down to Saint Bart. It was nice, except my mom spent the entire time stalking me at the pool, brandishing this tube of sunscreen with like SPF 87. Basically I read a lot, listened to my iPod, and wrote in my journal – just dumb poems about water and fish, and what it's like to fall asleep in the sun and wake up thinking you're in heaven. The drums? A band? Nothing was further from my mind.

Until I was back at school, and Stella Saunders was literally auditioning on air bass for me in homeroom. And that was very shocking, because Stella was . . . she was . . . I was not her type. Suddenly, though, the band thing didn't seem so stupid anymore. Stella's in the top 10 percentile at school. And she is *driven*. So that's when I got a practical thought: If I had a band with Stella Saunders, it would be serious; she would really do it.

She leaned over my desk and rattled my arm. 'Yo, Barbie,' she said. 'Don't sleep. You got some hot-shit entertainment lawyer telling you he could make you the next big thing and you're like, "Ohhh, I don't know . . ."'

I started to feel a little uncomfortable. Stella was talking loud. People were turning around to stare at us.

'Excuse me?' Stella kind of growled at this girl in the row in front of us. With her huge eyes shooting lightning sparks and that thundercloud of hair, Stella can be scary.

The girl turned around, and Stella got back to me, huddling in close and putting her arm around me. This made me feel … I don't know, a million different ways, some of them very unusual, most of them very good. Her breath on my neck — warm and scented from that lavender-violet gum she likes — it gave me the chills.

'Come on,' Stella said, squeezing my shoulders.

'This could be *amazing*.' Then she let go and fell back in her seat, making the chair lurch and squeak. 'You make me so mad!' she said. 'You're just like all the rest of these rich-ass Bergdorf-Goodman bitches who don't ever have to *do* anything.'

I could not speak. Literally, my mouth was frozen. My tongue was just this foreign object. My mind was racing — but I could not say a thing to this girl. And she just sat there, staring at me like I was the world's biggest, fattest stupid person. I thought I would cry, but I really, really did not want to cry. I wanted Stella Saunders to know that I was not like that! And she kept staring at me, tilted back in her chair with her arms crossed over her chest. I don't know how long it was until I did manage to get something out, but eventually I did. I said, 'I am not.'

'I am not!' Stella mimicked me. 'Not what?'

'I'm sorry. I don't know but — I am *not* like that.'

Then the bell rang, and Stella jumped up and grabbed her books and was like, 'Whatever, dude.' I sat there for half a second and then I bolted up too and grabbed my stuff; I followed her out into the hall. I caught up to her and touched her arm. With a flip of her shoulder she spun around and was like, 'WHAT!?'

Everything about Stella right then – her wide-legged stance, her slit-eyed glare – was meant to scare me, but I held my ground. That was a good feeling, and it kind of made time stand still.

'Look, you wanna say something to me, Wynn Morgan?' she said. 'Because if not, step off – I'm gonna be late for Spanish.' Then she gave me that 'I'm *waiting . . .*' look.

'I just want to say . . .' I paused to see if she was even listening, and she was. 'I just want to say that I am *not* lazy or any of those things you said, but the thing is I don't even know how to play drums.'

Stella goes, 'So? *Learn.*' And then she turned around and walked away.

I don't want to make it sound like Stella talked me into it – it was more like she challenged me, and no one had ever done that before. So that afternoon I told my mom I wanted to take lessons on the drums. Immediately, she picked up the phone to call my stepdad's office, but she didn't ask for him. Instead she said, 'Give me Brian Wandweiler.'

I started lessons the next day, with this guy Travis Brown who's a legendary session player. He doesn't really even give lessons, he was just doing a favour for Mr Wandweiler – Brian. My mom brought me downtown to Travis's studio; she sat in the lounge with her cell phone and her *Vogue,* and Travis took me into this other room. And . . . there it was – a drum kit, a massive one. Suddenly I got very nervous. The good thing was,

I'd never heard of Travis Brown before – knowing what a big deal he is would have made me even more nervous.

Either Travis didn't notice how freaked I was, or he pretended not to. We went over the basics: Here's how to hold the sticks. This is the kick drum, and here's how you hit it with your foot. Here's the snare, here's the tom-tom. He was so not patronizing about it. Plus, he wasn't looking at me in that way older guys – men – usually do, like they're trying *not* to look; I hate that. So all that kind of calmed me down.

Then he goes, 'Look, Wynn, there's a lot to learn about playing the drums, but there's one thing you can't learn – you got to be born with it. And I'm not about to waste my time with you if you don't have it.'

I had no clue what 'it' was, but I said, 'All right.'

He dimmed the lights and left me alone. For a whole minute I just sat there. Then I hit the cymbal softly – it rang with a shivery ring. I used my foot on the pedal. The kick drum thumped – louder than I thought it would, but bigger than the sound was the feeling: very powerful. I tapped the sticks on the snare – in the middle, on the rim. Then I sat some more and breathed. It was almost dark in the room and chilly and very, very quiet. I could hear my heart and my breath; it was like I could hear my *teeth,* my *skin.*

And I thought, well, I could just start flailing, but somehow that seemed, I don't know, disrespectful. Instead, I tried to think up a rhythm, and a really simple one came to me: thump-thump-*pop,* thump-thump-*pop,* thump-thump-pop-pop; thump-thump-*pop.* I whispered it to myself, and then I began to play it. I played it a few times, and then I played it faster, and

19

then I added a cymbal crash, and, well, I don't know how long I was at it but suddenly the lights in the studio came up, and Travis, who was behind the glass in the booth the whole time, started smacking on the window and waving and making the thumbs-up sign. Then his voice came through the speakers and he was like, 'Oh yes, young lady, you *are* going to play the drums!'

The whole thing, I don't know . . . it validated me. Plus, I always *felt* music, I mean really felt it as a physical *feeling,* as much as I got into the lyrics on a mental level, but before that day I had no way to express that, even acknowledge it. That day I did something with my soul that made me sweat and smile, and it just kind of clicked.

We went to get me my kit the next day. The icky guy in the music store tried to talk us into these top-of-the-line DWs, but I didn't care that they were the most expensive drums in the place. But there was this really nice Pearl kit in a soft pink colour. Which was ironic because drums are big and loud yet these were sweet, so I picked them.

We set them up in this room at the far end of the first floor of our townhouse. It would be a maid's room but isn't because my mom thinks live-in help is ostentatious, plus I think she thinks it's creepy – she doesn't want people living in her house; I can't even have a cat – so the room was just being used for storage. After school, every day, I'd go down and practise. I wasn't good, but more important than how good I was, or wasn't, was that I had found something, I had really, really found something and it felt really, really good.

The Boss

Look, I know we're supposed to tell every juicy little detail, all right, but in the beginning it was just practise and music lessons and, trust, that is a snore. Hmm, well, a couple of interesting things did happen early on. Like going to Wynn's house for the first time and seeing how freakin' rich she really is. See, Wynn does not dress all tricked-out with a lot of logos or bling. But we are talking muh-nee. Her stepdad is an über-lawyer and the mom comes from money, 'old' money.

Their house isn't much bigger than ours, but they don't have any tenants, they live in the whole place. See, I know about this stuff because my mom is an estate agent and she's always saying *location, location, location.* Well, Wynn's house is definitely located, located, located on the snooty Upper East Side.

I go in there, feeling like I wanna big-up her mom: 'Props to you, Mrs Sherman!' (Sherman is her last name now; Wynn's last name is Morgan, from her real dad.) But I know how to talk to parents. I was very polite and demure. I think I've always known there are different ways you have to talk to different people. And let me tell you: In the music business it's like that to the tenth power. You gotta be very careful what you say and how you say

21

it to who. Anyway, we had 'refreshments' in the 'nook' and then went out to the 'servant's quarters' where Wynn's kit is. We messed around trying to play along to the Ramones' *Blitzkrieg Bop*.

'Oh, man, we suck!' I said after a while. 'Like a vacuum cleaner. Like a groupie on a tour bus.'

Wynn got up and started to pace the little room. 'Maybe we should call it off.'

And I was like, 'Are you crazy? No freakin' way!' I shook my head. 'What, do rich people think everything is just gonna happen like that?' I said with a snap. 'You thought we were gonna go "one, two, three, four," and just know what we were doing?'

'No, no, no,' Wynn said, that too-long fringe of hers hiding her eyes. 'I don't expect it to come easy. But I don't want Mr Wandweilder to go, "What was I thinking?"'

She was talking about our meeting with her stepdad's partner.

'Not gonna happen,' I told her. 'Not if you sit your ass down and shut up. Come on, you count it off . . .'

And Wynn smiled and sat down and clacked her sticks: 'One, two, three, *four!*'

But I won't front: I was nervous to meet Brian. If he was cool with us, something was gonna happen – and if he was not, it would be *buh*-bye! So I didn't know how to act. It was driving me bananas. I asked Wynn what he was like but she was no help; she was just like 'I don't know – I guess he's nice.' Useless.

We were gonna have lunch before we played for him. I was freaking out about my outfit, my hair – which I never do. And

I was thinking I wouldn't be able to eat – and I am so not that girl; I can always eat. Worse, I thought the restaurant was gonna be all stuffy, and the waiters would give my punk gear and electro-fro that 'what are youuuuu doing here?' look. But it was a very low-key diner on Ninth Avenue. When I walked in the waitress was just like, 'One?' and I didn't see Wynn so I told her I was meeting two other people. She put me in a booth and handed me this old-school record album – an LP, right? I was like 'what the . . .' but I opened it and the menu was inside, so I figured out that's why they call the place Vynl, and that was very cool.

So I'm looking at the menu when I hear someone say, 'Hey . . . are you Stella?' I glance up and *bang!* Right from that *second,* from the sound of my name in his mouth, from the second I looked in his eyes, I knew. It was gonna be OK, better than OK. I could just tell – and he could too. Our connection was instan-freakin'-taneous. It didn't matter that he's some white guy twice my age. That's why I hate stereotypes – you just can't have any because you never know when you're gonna meet someone who is the complete opposite from you on the outside, but on the inside just *gets* you. The two of us, Brian and I, we are simpatico. I love that word. *Simpatico.*

By the time Wynn walks in ten minutes late because she couldn't get a cab – I'm coming all the way from Sunset freakin' Park and I'm early, all right? – Brian and I have ordered the same drink (lemonade). We're talking about our favourite bands, and when I tell him it irks me that people think I should only be into R&B and rap because I'm black, he starts smiling and nodding his head. He knows exactly what I mean because he's a New York Jew and he's supposed to be into rock and, now, hip-hop because all middle-class white people are into hip-hop, but what he really loves is country.

Now this put me off a teeny bit. 'Country? You mean Shania Twain?'

He winces and shakes his head vehemently, making his hair flop around and his glasses slip down his nose. 'I mean *real* country – the masters. Johnny Cash. Waylon Jennings…' His eyes behind the glasses are honest eyes – wide, amber brown and almost liquid-y, translucent. He pushes his specs back in place. 'Lorretta Lynn. The Louvin Brothers.'

Names I never even heard, all right.

And he says, 'The point is, you never know what is going to sing to you – to *you* – unless you look for it and open yourself up to it and give it a chance.'

That was the single most beautiful piece of advice anyone has ever given me.

Anyway, Wynn sits down and we eat lunch and if it bothers her how much Brian and I are vibing she doesn't get weird. We talk a little bit about what kind of band we're going to be, but not much. After, Brian asks if we mind walking to the rehearsal space – I'm thinking I wouldn't mind walking straight off a bridge for this guy right now. Trouble is, I'm freezing my ass off. A killer wind blows at us off the Hudson River, and my 'impress the impresario' outfit includes a short kilt and torn-up fishnet tights. Finally we get to a crappy-looking building but I'm just glad to get inside. The lift wheezes its way up, and Brian leads us into this … box. A tiny room, dark, fifty years' worth of cigarette stink imbedded in the industrial grey carpet. A duct-taped drum kit and some dilapidated amps huddle like homeless men who've found makeshift shelter from the cold. This is a rehearsal studio? Not very rock-star glam. I don't know if it's creeping Wynn out but I quickly get over myself and think, *Yeah. Keep it real.*

Well, we put the Ramones CD on, and Wynn and I struggle to get through the two songs we've 'mastered.' Brian is watching and when we stop he explains to us what a rhythm section really is. How we need each other and feed each other and how we will ultimately do that for the rest of the band, that you can have all the fancy singers and flash guitar players in the world but they are useless without us. We are the bones of the band. Then he asks us to play the songs again but wants me to stand in a different place, so that Wynn and I can see each other and have a real musical communication. I was like, 'whatever,' but I am telling you, it makes a huge difference.

The thing I liked best about that day was that every time we did our thing, Brian did not clap. He talked to us straight up. He's professional, and that's how he treated us. Afterwards, when we went to sit on this lumpy sofa in front of the lift, he broke it down like this: 'This is what I see: two hot girls who want to rock out and have fun. And there is definitely an audience for that. Now it's a question of what you'll develop into.'

He started going off on this whole philosophical soliloquy of modern music and pop culture, and we just sat there, gaping, listening like he was the rock-and-roll Socrates or some shit. Then he talked about what we could bring to the mix, throwing words like 'exuberance' and 'naïveté' and 'passion' all over the place.

'So here's what we're going to do,' he said. 'You guys are going to practise your asses off. Wynn, I talked Travis into spending a little more time with you. Twice a week, you take lessons. Stella, you too: twice a week. I'll e-mail you the names of a few teachers. Tell your parents the firm is paying – it's an investment. When you're not taking lessons, you practise. Every day for at least two hours. OK?'

Wynn and I looked at each other and back at him, nodding like a couple of Bobble Heads.

'Good. Now here's what *I'm* going to do. I'm going to get out there and find you two things – a ringer and a singer.'

The Boy

All along, Brian Wandweilder was planning to put a chick band together, but when he heard me play, the lightbulb went on over his head. He realized adding a boy would make us different — obviously — from other chick bands. Maybe he also thought I would lend some cred, or make us more media-worthy. Mostly I think he was just sick of the chicks he was seeing. The ones that could shred were old — like, twenty-three — and the ones that were cute and young could not play a lick.

The dickwad who was allegedly managing me at the time had heard what Wandweilder was up to, but he didn't think it was right for me; he thought it was manufactured and phony. But I was like, 'manufacture *this!*' because he wasn't exactly setting me up with tons of auditions or label meetings or anything. So I decided to outsmart him. I peeked at his Palm Pilot for the guy, Gaylord Kramer, who had told him about Wandweilder's master plan. I called Gaylord, introduced myself, and told him I wanted to go for it.

Gaylord called himself a manager but he was hardly connected up the wazoo. He didn't even have an office, but he had a cell phone, so he'd sit in Washington Square and try to get his clients the hookup from a park bench. He was hungry, a real hustler, and the first time I met him he was wearing a 'Mean People Suck Evil People' T-shirt, so what was not to like?

Anyway, there I was, hanging out on the bench with Gaylord. Now, it was a fluke that he even *heard* about what Wandweilder was doing. For Gaylord, just getting a major player like Brian on the phone took three days of constant pestering. But I was there when he finally got through, and he was hyping me like I was the bastard child of Tchaikovsky and Eddie Van Halen with a touch of Jack White. So Gaylord finally says, 'But listen, Brian – A/B is as pretty as a girl.'

I wasn't liking that too much. I figured a straight guy called Gaylord would feel my pain, but, um, no.

'Scruffy, sexy, sweet,' Gaylord said into his cell. 'Member of the tribe, I think.' He put his hand over the phone, 'Hey!' he hissed at me. 'You bar mitzvahed?'

I nodded.

'Yeah, bar mitzvah boy with perfect skin, curly locks, and pouty lips.'

I touched my lips. Were they pouty?

'He's a beautiful kid. Girls all over America will go wango-tango – that is a promise. And he can play. I mean, *playyyy,* man. He's classically trained: keyboards, guitar, you want banjo, cello, whatever . . .'

Suddenly I had an audition. It all happened so quick, I didn't have time to get overly intimidated. Gaylord must have been confident because he sprang for a cab up to Wandweilder's office. I walked in, and Wandweilder looked like an OK guy – younger than I expected, average height, little wire glasses, and, surprisingly, no suit – so that took the edge off. We shook hands, but didn't do small talk. He had a little Peavey amp in the corner of his office and I plugged in, tuned up, and proceeded to blow his argyles onto Fifth Avenue.

The Voice

I am so, so, so, so blessed! This has all been a dream come true. Every day is another prayer answered. It's hard to believe that my mom was even the littlest bit unsure about the whole thing. Yes, she is my 'momager.'

I guess she was just being extra careful. This is my career and all. Also, I think she always imagined that I'd be a solo artist – a Britney Spears, only not trashy. Or if not a pop star, then someone like LeAnn Rimes, because we both love country music. So does Mr Wandweilder – we all bonded over that. Mr Wandweilder says he's going to get us to meet Willie Nelson, one of our favourite country stars. Can you imagine? My mom would just about faint!

Personally, I never listened to a lot of rock and roll before. I listened mostly to the radio stations my mom liked. At talent shows, I'd perform Faith Hill and Celine Dion songs, stuff that really let me showcase my vocals. And I did get lots of attention, because we found a producer to do a demo for me. Except he and my mom butted heads over material – that producer wanted me to do some R&B pop-type songs because that was what was selling, but my mom doesn't like that kind of music.

So we got burned: He kept all our money, even though we only got a three-song demo instead of a five-song one. That's why my mom was sceptical when Mr Wandweilder, who'd got a hold of my demo, asked us to take a meeting.

The first thing Mr Wandweilder said to us after offering us water or coffee or soda or anything, anything at all, was: 'Kendall Taylor, can you rock out or what?'

My mom was like, 'Excuse me?'

He just laid it on the line for us. He was putting together a rock band with teens in it, and one way to make it special was to have a lead singer who could *really* sing. Because so many rock girls were screamers, or too nasal, or too breathy. He stood up from his desk and told us he knew he had to have me in this band after he heard my demo. He said he believed I had only tapped a part of what my voice could do. Yes, I had range, but I also had dimension, 'unfathomable' dimension. Voices within the voice. There was something of the preacher to Mr Wandweilder that day. Every word he said, I could have sopped up with a biscuit – but my mom thought it was crazy talk.

'Excuse me, Mr Wandweilder,' she said. 'You need to slow down a minute.'

He got all quiet and dipped his head. Then he glanced up and sighed and sat back down. 'You're right,' he said. 'I'm sorry, Mrs Taylor. I'm sorry, Kendall. I got carried away, but you're right.' He sipped some water out of a blue bottle. 'There's no way this would work out for Kendall.'

Oh my sweet lord! When he said that I felt like I had just gotten up the nerve to climb the high diving board and someone had let all the water out of the pool.

31

Mr Wandweilder looked at my mom and said, 'Kendall is very innocent, isn't she, Mrs Taylor? And that innocence is something you want to preserve and protect as long as possible, am I right?'

My mom opened her mouth, but then she shut it and he went on. 'Well, I don't want to break your hearts, but someone has got to tell you before you get in too deep. This industry eats innocence for breakfast. So go.' He pointed towards his office door. 'Go now. Because I think, yes, Kendall could give this band the special magic ingredient that could make it skyrocket. But what would being in the band do to Kendall? Twist her, hurt her in some way? I don't want that responsibility. So I say "go." Go now. Sing in the shower. Sing in church. But stay away from "the business" – it's hell.'

Then he just sat there and looked at us. A chokyburny feeling rose up in my throat. I didn't know where to look – at him, at my mom, at all the gold and platinum records hanging in his office. First he was telling me I was perfect, then he was saying I was all wrong. I didn't know what to think, or say.

Thank goodness my mom did. 'I see, Mr Wandweilder,' she began in the tight, quiet voice she only uses when she's mad. 'We appreciate you taking the time to meet with us. But' – I could tell by the 'but' that my mom had a few things to tell Mr Brian Wandweilder. She said she doubted that he'd ever met any Southern women before, because Southern women are genteel on the outside but steel on the inside and nobody, *nobody,* eats a Southern woman for breakfast, lunch, or dinner.

By the time she was done, I was in the band.

Mr Wandweilder took my e-mail address so he could send

me some MP3s – I should practise the songs I liked. *Some* MP3s? Gosh, those songs started coming in a flood. Classic rock, old soul, alternative artists. Every generation from the fifties till now. Songs by Sonic Youth, Dusty Springfield, Jimi Hendrix, The Cars, Iggy Pop, Tom Petty, Nirvana, Led Zeppelin, Janis Joplin, Guided by Voices, Velvet Underground, Mudhoney, Fugazi, Rolling Stones, Beach Boys, The Beatles … There was so much to listen to, so much to learn. It's not that I'd never heard rock music – gosh, I don't think you can be fifteen and go to school or the mall and not be exposed to it. But I'd never *experienced* it before. So it was a whole ear-opening discovery for me. And discovering rock and roll was like discovering chocolate . . . and chocolate sure is good.

The Boy

I'd like to say that everything went down smoothly the first time we all got together. I'd like to say that I was chill, with a real 'hey, ladies, how you doing' vibe. I'd like to say that – but it would be a lie. That first meeting? Nightmare!

The trouble started before I even got there. I know my way around the city well enough to find the rehearsal space Brian had booked for us, easy. It was close to Penn Station, and since I was early when I got off the train, I thought I'd mellow out a little with this weed I copped off a guy in fifth period PE that day. Well, I have to say my man was definitely into another realm of quality there, because by the time I reached the studio, I was mighty buzzed.

First thing I see when I get off the elevator is Brian talking to this lady who is obviously, even to me, in my altered state, somebody's mom. This makes me go, 'huh?' because Brian spoke to all the nice moms and dads on the phone to explain the no-parents policy at rehearsals. Suddenly I get that 'uh-oh' feeling.

Brian sees me and right off he goes: 'A/B! Oh, look, Mrs Taylor, it's A/B. Isn't that great, you'll get to meet A/B at least before you leave.'

Bad idea, Brian. But I shuffle over anyway and then Brian sees it is a bad idea too. My eyes are bloodshot and for all I know there's a piece of sweet leaf stuck between my two front teeth. Brian had spent the last twenty minutes convincing Mrs Taylor to leave her daughter in his care, then I march in smelling like Snoop Dogg's personal grow room.

But what can he do? Here I am in all my stoner glory. So he goes: 'A/B, this is Mrs Taylor — her daughter, Kendall, is that remarkable singer I've told you so much about.'

'Hey,' I said. I guess I forgot to put out my hand for her to shake, because Brian elbowed me, and I thrust it at her. She was a real lady — she took it even though she probably would have preferred the decomposing corpse of a New York City subway rat.

'A/B is our guitarist,' said Brian. 'He also plays keyboards, and, well, he's truly a very talented young man.'

I gave my sheepish grin, pulling up my guitar case to eye level so she'd see he wasn't lying. Of course for all she knew I had two kilos in there.

'Nice to meet you; I'm JoBeth Taylor,' she said. 'A/B? Is that your name?'

Why, oh why, didn't I simply say 'uh-huh' and be out of there? The poor woman just seemed mystified over why my insane, irresponsible parents hadn't given me a proper name. So I went into my spiel. 'Well, you know Jews — gotta name your kid after the dearly departed, right? I'm Abraham, for my dead grandfather, and Benjamin, for my dead great-uncle. But Abraham Benjamin Farrelberg — a mouthful, I know. So for short, I honour both dead relatives. Only here's the thing —

instead of A-period, B-period, I do it with a slash, no periods. You know, like AC/DC?'

Kendall's mom did not know, not at all. Her bottom lip was quivering like Elvis's left leg. Right then, Brian got on damage control: 'Why don't you go on into the studio, A/B? Room four. There's some snacks in there, and you can introduce yourself to Kendall.'

'Snacks,' I said, nodding and smiling. 'Cool.' I gave them the thumbs-up. Then I leaned in towards Brian and whispered, 'Brian, umm, sorry, but . . . I really need to take a whiz . . .'

He gripped my shoulder and gave me a wise, Yodalike look. 'Bathroom's right over there, down the hall, make a left.'

I started for it.

'A *left*, A/B . . .' Brian called after me.

The Voice

I am a very open-minded and friendly person. So the first time I saw A/B, I went right over and said, 'Hi! I'm Kendall Taylor! I sing!' But that boy just passed right by me and headed straight for this folding table. He grabbed a green Gatorade and said, 'Ugh,' then drank half of it down, said, 'Ugh' again, and finished it. Then he looked at me for the first time. 'Sorry,' he said. 'Cotton mouth.' I must have cocked my head, like, *What in the world is he talking about?* But then he smiled, and A/B just has the most beautiful smile.

Even though he's shaggy-looking and wasn't neatly dressed, I realized A/B was awfully cute in that skinny rock-and-roll boy way. With the kind of hair that's all messy and sticking up in spots, and the skinny peglegged jeans and all. And skin I bet never had a pimple on it ever. He surveyed all the snacks, then turned to me and said, 'Zagnut?'

The way he said it made me giggle. I went over to the table and told him, 'I'm more of an Almond Joy girl myself. Or Butterfinger.'

'Yeah? Like Bart Simpson?' he said. 'Where do you stand on the Kit Kat?'

He just made it so easy to talk to him. I don't have much experience with boys, and while I'm really not self-conscious about my weight – we are all God's creatures and if one person is a little bit chubby she should be all right with that – sometimes around boys a person can start wondering if the boy isn't thinking about God's plan but thinking that the girl is fat. But A/B just seemed nice, so I said, 'I like them,' about the Kit Kats. Then I asked, 'Hey, have you ever had a deep-fried Snickers?'

'Oh, please, do not tell me that such a thing even exists!' He put up his hands like, *Stop!* 'In my condition I don't think I could handle it!'

At the time I didn't know what A/B meant by 'my condition,' but now I know. He was referring to the fact that he was high on marijuana, and when a person is high on marijuana they sometimes crave sweets because the TCH, which is the active ingredient in the marijuana, makes the blood sugar go down. This is what is commonly known as the munchies. A few months ago, I went on a website to learn all about it, since I think it's nice to show interest in things people you like are interested in, and A/B is very interested in marijuana. But I did not know that then, so I just ignored that part of what he said.

Right about then, Stella Saunders and Wynn Morgan walked in. We heard them before we saw them, since Stella announced, 'We're here!' really loud. A/B turned to look at her, but then he looked at Wynn, because, well, people can't help looking at Wynn. I looked at her too. Even though she was only wearing jeans and a sweater, they were not like *my* jeans and a sweater. Gosh, at the time I did not know there was such a thing as two-hundred-dollar blue jeans, but I definitely knew there was something about Wynn's blue jeans that was not like mine. Her haircut looked expensive too – long and very messy, but not A/B messy; it was the kind of messy you pay for; plus it was about seven different shades of blond all blended in to look very natural.

I guess Stella was used to having Wynn automatically get attention, so she knew how to steal it back. She shrugged her bass off and leaned it down carefully, then bent over at the hips to pull off her knitted cap and shake out this wild head of hair. After that, she took off her leather jacket in a noisy, dramatic way and flung it on the floor. The room was so dingy, with nothing in it but amps and cables and cords, and it smelled terribly stale. But somehow, with Stella there, suddenly it felt like the place to be.

Stella sashayed over to us, with Wynn trailing behind her. Wynn's taller than all of us, even taller than A/B by an inch, but she was still in Stella's shadow. She hadn't said a single thing yet.

Stella pointed at me and said, 'Singer!' Then she pointed at A/B, 'Ringer!'

Behind her Wynn laughed in a soft way. If it was a joke, A/B and I didn't get it.

Then Wynn said, 'Don't mind Stella. She's just obnoxious; she can't help it.' I could tell right then that she was nice. 'I'm Wynn,' she said.

'I'm Kendall Taylor,' I said. 'I've been looking forward to meeting both of you.'

Then the three of us girls looked at A/B, waiting for him to introduce himself, but he was staring at Wynn, his eyes glazed like a country ham. She coughed as if to break the spell, startling A/B, who realized we were all waiting on him.

'I'm Body,' he blurted. 'Sorry, sorry! I mean, I'm A/B.'

The Body

Thank God for Stella. When A/B accidentally introduced himself as 'Body,' she had my back, stepping up and snapping her fingers in his face. 'Yo!' she said. 'They are just tits. Juggs. Knockers. Fun bags. If we're gonna be in a band together, you'd better get over it. Them. Now.'

There's really nothing like having someone jump to your defence. And even though Stella can come off cold, being around her makes me feel, I don't know, protected I guess. Safe.

Well, Brian must have thought we'd had enough 'getting to know you' time because he came in, clapping his hands and going, 'Enough of your yakking – let's get down to business.' That's when reality struck – and turned us into zombies. Now that it was time to start playing together, we were all suddenly awkward. Maybe we were waiting for Brian to give us direction, but he just hung back. We were like people on the subway when it stops between stations, standing around, studying each other's feet.

Then, out of nowhere, Kendall walks up to the mike. She makes a *pfft* sound to test it, and then she starts singing by herself. And it's not like she goes into *Kumbaya* or some nice

41

pretty song – she belts out the opening to AC/DC's *Back in Black*. 'BAAACK in BLAAACK!' But it's not a scream like how Brian Johnson does it; it's this deep, hot, beautiful thing.

All of us stare at her in disbelief – after all, Brian had told us Kendall wasn't really a rock chick and AC/DC is no easy listening. Well, I guess she'd been studying those MP3s he'd been sending us. Then A/B, who's a classic rock freak, scrambles for his guitar to accompany her. And even though we've never played the tune, it's fairly basic, beat-wise, so Stella and I go for it too and we all finish the song together. Miserably – but together. Sort of shy, sort of excited, our glances ricochet from one to the other. We're all sharing the same feeling, the one you get at a magic show, and the magician hasn't really done anything yet, but you know something amazing is definitely about to happen.

The Boss

I do not impress easy, all right, I just don't. But Kendall's voice? I can't even tell you. First of all, it's so amazing and second you just don't imagine it coming out of her. That little round moon-pie face, the baby fat, and – I am just being honest – she looks like she's got her shoes on the wrong feet. And not for nothing, but she's so white. Then she opens her mouth and she blows like a black girl. No, a black woman, a big black woman. And what does she belt out? 'Back in freakin' Black!'

I try not to let how good she is hold me back – I step up and start slapping my Mustang. That's the bass Brian bought me. One day, he was just like 'here;' no big deal. But I looove how it fits me perfectly – my brother's big bass was ridiculous on me – and I play ten times better with it. Plus, they don't even make them anymore; it's *vintage*. And I love that it's from Brian.

Anyway, after we finish massacring 'Back in Black,' Brian tells us to pull out our homework assignments – a list of our favourite ten songs from all the MP3s he's been sending us. Then he tells me to cover Kendall's eyes. *Huh?* I think, but I do it. He hands Wynn a marker, and tells A/B to hold one of our lists in front of Kendall. 'OK, Kendall, pick,' he says. She giggles and points at a song, Wynn marks it. We do this three more times, rotating who gets to pick, and those four songs become our set list. Whack as the whole pin-the-tail-on-the-donkey routine is, it's just another example of Brian's genius. No crybaby arguments over what to play — it's decided, bam. And of course it made sense to do random covers. At that stage in the game, we weren't a bona fide band yet. We were like chemicals thrown in a test tube, a lab experiment. Plus, I personally thought it was cool to take a bunch of songs your older brother or maybe even your parents would know, then tweak them into something unrecognizable, completely new. And, truth? Note-for-note covers were out of the question; we weren't good enough to sound like the originals.

So — drum roll or whatever — our songs: *Dirty Boots* by Sonic Youth, *You're All I've Got Tonight* by The Cars, *The Waiting* by Tom Petty, and *Teenage FBI* by Guided by Voices. That last one's from my list of faves; I'd never heard of GBV before Brian turned me on to them but now I looove them.

Brian opens his laptop. He's got it all tricked out with this new software that isn't even on the market yet, but when you click on a song in your library, it brings up the lyrics and chord changes. Half a minute later, Brian prints out copies of *Dirty Boots* for us, then downloads it through the speakers so we can have a listen. I'm all juiced to play it, and it looks like Wynn and A/B are too, but Kendall is reading the lyrics and freaking out. 'Excuse me, excuse me,' she says, her eyes darting all over the room. 'Mr Wandweilder, I *cannot* sing these words!' Our chunky little cherub has a problem with that 'Satan's got her tongue' line, but Brian takes her aside, and I don't know what he says but she comes back all talked into it.

We play it all the way through and it's a hot mess. So we have to keep playing it, over and over. We do it in chunks – first the intro, then we work on the verse, then we hone the chorus. Brian tells A/B he's in charge (makes sense – he's the virtuoso) and leaves the room to take care of other business on his cell. Gaylord pops his head in once – he's the guy who brought A/B to the band, but he works for us now, setting up lessons and booking rehearsals, since Brian's too busy and important for day-to-day grunt work.

Once our time's up, Brian comes in and goes, 'OK, band meeting!' So we file onto the lumpy sofa, and he tells us all to exchange digits, e-mail addresses – all the pertinent data. Then he says, 'But don't contact each other this weekend. In fact, I don't want you to practise or even think about music for forty-eight hours. You have to promise me that you'll have a normal weekend – hang out, do whatever it is you normally do with yourselves. And *enjoy* it. Then think about this: How much will you miss this normal stuff – and can you deal with that? Because it's pretty much going to stop the next time you all get together. *If* you all get together.'

Before we could collectively groan, Brian held up his hand. 'Look, I'm not about to give you guys some empty pep talk here – I'm a lawyer, not a cheerleader,' he said. 'But I know bands, and I'll tell you this: The ones that make it *need* to make it. Sure, talent helps . . .' He was looking at Kendall and A/B. 'Good looks, style, a definite plus.' That was with his focus on Wynn. 'Attitude, absolutely, a rock and roll requirement.' You

45

know it was all about me then. 'But you can have all that, and chemistry besides, but without the drive, the commitment, the failure-is-not-an-option ethos, you're not getting out of the garage . . . or the crappy West Side rehearsal space.' Brian studied each of us in turn again, calculating the hunger in our eyes. 'One other thing: Since this is supposed to be a band, you've all got to be in it a hundred and ten percent . . . *together.*'

And I'm thinking: *I feel you, Brian. I know you want us to be sure we can commit to this. But no matter what, I'm gonna do this. Now I got my taste – my tunes, my Mustang, and you, Mr Brian Wandweilder – I'm in. I am in.*

The Boss

So we were supposed to have an ordinary, average weekend.
Fine. This was my agenda: Sleep late, eat Lucky Charms,
study for this biology test, and oh, yeah – lose my virginity.
That's right, Mom and Dad, too bad you might be finding out
about this with the rest of America, but here's how it is: I didn't
have sex because I'm out of control or chemically depressed or
making some passive-aggressive cry for your attention. What I
did – what I do – really has nothing to do with you. Hasn't
since I was about five. I love and respect you and blah-blah-
blah, but you guys got out of the picture pretty early.

Which makes me normal. All right, maybe some kids do shit
just to drive their parents crazy, or pay their parents back for
driving *them* crazy. But mostly kids do shit, whether it's sex or
drugs or piercing or whatever, because we wanna do it. It's that
simple. Feed us, try not to drop us on our head too many times,
and set a good example because we cannot stand hypocrisy.
Other than that, please leave us alone. We have things to do. We
are not possessed by the devil – we are just living our lives.

When it came to sex, I was curious. On a pure science level:
What does it feel like to have it inside you? But I was never in

a rush. Not because I was waiting to fall in love. The *last* person I wanted to lose my virginity to was someone I loved, because when we broke up it'd be extra painful. Besides, shit, I wanna be *good* at sex by the time I'm in love. I don't wanna be some dumb-ass little virgin who does not know what to do with a penis. Plus, that whole lay-down-and-die-for-me kind of love? I don't even know if that's my thing. Ninety-nine point nine percent of the female population might disagree, but to Ms Point One Percent — aka me — it just seems corny. Not to mention crazy. Juliet Capulet was a freak and a half.

Anyway, suddenly, that weekend, I got in a hurry. I felt like I was starting out on this whole next level of life and being a virgin just didn't go with that. So I decided to get with one of my guy friends. I had plenty to pick from, since I have more guy friends than girl friends. Everything's so much simpler with boys — you can just hang out, you don't have to get so *involved*. Still, I pretty much knew straight up it was gonna be Tee.

I'd already made out with him and . . . put it this way: When I made out with him, I felt it down there, even though I did not let him touch me down there. Plus, Tee didn't have a big mouth — he would not spread my business all over the neighbourhood. I believed this because I'd heard he had done it with this other girl, and I did *not* hear it from him. Also, not to stereotype, but Tee is Latin and everyone knows Latin guys are good in bed.

That Saturday was a party at this girl's house — her mother was away somewhere. If everything went right, I would lose my virginity to Tee on her mother's bed.

I get there late, and I'm rolling solo; I go up to Tee and we're talking. That's when I tell him that this is his lucky night — then

I walk away without another word. Kind of mysterious. Let him *think* on it. I go talk to some other kids I know from the block. People are smoking and drinking; not everybody, but, hey, it's a party. There's some beer, a bottle of Kahlua. But I just say no because I don't want to get shit-faced – I want to remember this. Then I give Tee the look until he works his way over to me. I tell him, 'Come with me, I wanna show you something.' We go into the girl's mother's bedroom and I pull out the condoms I bought that day. So Tee just smiles and, well, that's all I'm gonna say. I'm not gonna give any details and make this like porn or anything.

All right, I will say this: Pay attention if they show you how to use condoms in your health class, because I didn't and neither did Tee, and we wasted half the package. The other thing I'm gonna say is: It gets better the more you do it. Over the next month or so I had sex with Tee five times and it kept getting better. Although it didn't take long till I was over him. He started to kind of *expect* sex, and I was like: I am not your girlfriend, I am not your slave, I got other shit on my mind, so *please;* That's what I thought – but I was nicer about it to his face, and we went back to being just friends.

Anyway, that night, after I accomplished my mission, I felt different. I felt like, all right, whatever happens next I'm ready. Also, I felt good knowing that this was *my* game – no boy conned me into it, it didn't 'just happen' in some stoned, drunk moment of stupidity. I was proud in a way, and I wanted to keep it mine. I didn't have the urge to call anyone and be like: 'Guess what? I just had *SEX*.' I'm saying it now because, damn, it is so easy for me to talk in front of a camera. Some people probably get scared and clam up. But the fact is, A) I have no fear, and B) I've always known I'd be famous – I've been practising doing talk shows and shit since I was little. But I never told anyone before.

When I got home that night I went straight for the Lucky Charms but they didn't taste good to me any more. Weird.

The Body

If anyone wasn't going back to the band after a weekend of blissful slacking . . . um, you're looking at her. Least talent, most work, that was the equation as I saw it. But it wasn't as simple as just saying 'buh-bye, band!' If I quit, the whole thing would fall apart and everyone would be mad, yet if I stayed they would have to contend with the most beat-challenged excuse for a drummer ever. How was I supposed to just be normal with that weighing on my mind? I decided to call Liv Curson, who I hadn't hung with in ages even though she was probably my closest friend. We'd go shopping, have our nails done – it would be a good distraction, I hoped. Strolling through the boutique mecca of Soho and Nolita, we spent a bunch of money on stupid stuff: candles, makeup, socks. Then Liv got some tops to take on spring break next month – she was going to see her real dad in LA. I considered calling my real dad; maybe I could visit him in Prague. He runs an international banking firm there.

A romantic notion – ooh, a continental holiday! – but a moronic one. The fact is, our relationship is about as substantial as toilet paper. He calls on the dot of New Year's Day and my birthday, and I can call him anytime . . . but my 'biological father,' who is he *really*? My mom was done with him when I was seven, telling me they'd 'grown apart.' At the time I was sad but my mom abhors moping, so I just got used to him being gone. Now we have dinner when he comes to New York and it's like talking to someone else's parent. Filling him in about me and the drums, the band thing . . . such an effort.

Liv wanted pizza so we went to this trattoria. Some NYU guys tried to pick us up. Technically hot – built, but not frat-thugs, studiously groomed facial hair – but I don't know, guys can be ... such *guys*. One of them kept asking if I was in the Victoria's Secret catalogue. Repulsive. Only Topher or Tanger or Lager, whatever his name was, he was nice and had good taste in music; we talked a while. He asked for my number and I gave him a fake one, which is what I always do. Even if a boy is nice – it's me, I'm defective, I chicken out. None of them asked for Liv's number, and I don't know if this upset her or not. Liv doesn't talk much about feelings.

That's so weird to me. Women are supposed to be emotional and expressive, just spouting, gushing geysers of feeling. Well, Liv isn't. Stella certainly isn't. My mom, the person I'm supposed to be heart-to-hearty with – ha. My mother discusses events but dismisses *why* things happen. To me, everything happens because of the why, but start talking about the why and my mom changes the subject.

After the NYU guys left, Liv was craving cannoli. She sucked out the cream, then ate the crust. I got a cappuccino. She asked me about the band, which was nice, but when I started telling her she seemed to zone out, so I stopped. Just then I knew Liv and I probably wouldn't be best friends forever. We had 'grown apart.' That made me, not sad . . . more sort of bittersweet. That feeling you get when the summer's almost over – not a pain but a ghost of a pain somewhere between your heart and your stomach? It was like that. In my mind I saw Liv and I walking away from each other someday, probably soon. But that day, we still went back uptown for manis and pedis.

My mom and stepdad were dining out that night and they didn't ask me to join them, which was OK. I'd shown my mom the stuff I'd bought that afternoon and to her that counts as 'bonding.' Once they left I thought I'd watch a movie, but first I went to look at my drums. Just stand outside the door and look at them. Was Brian testing us when he insisted 'no practising?' Was it one of those 'don't think of a green elephant' kind of things?

Standing there, I began to stress – about being in a band, playing drums . . . make that barely playing drums. About Brian expecting me to sing lead on 'You're All I've Got Tonight.' Singing while playing the drums is like a conversation between two people, one speaking Chinese and the other Lithuanian. Plus, I have a seriously unpretty voice. Brian said that didn't matter; I just had to be an *interesting* singer. Whatever that is. Sometimes I wonder what Brian's really got up his sleeve. Does he have a master plan for his little rock-and-roll puppets? Or is he just winging it right along with us? Maybe Brian had some loud fast dreams when he was a kid, but he quashed them and followed the rules – good grades, law school, partnership at a top firm. Only now those loud fast dreams are haunting him. So he's going back to live them out – taking chances, screwing around – through us. I don't know. It's just one more thing to obsess over.

Uch, I couldn't stand just standing there, so I ran to our library. My mom calls it that, and yes the walls are lined with books, but I can't remember anyone actually reading in there. It's really our home entertainment centre – a big plasma TV and tons of DVDs, so incongruous with all that lofty literature. I was about to pop in some neo-noir British indie fare when I noticed a yellow envelope on the coffee table with my name on it. Inside was a DVD, *The Kids Are Alright,* and a note from Brian – all it said was: Have fun! Fun was heavily underlined.

The DVD was about that English band The Who. It didn't take long before I figured out why Brian sent it over. The drummer from The Who – the original one, he's dead now, Keith Moon – I think he may have been the best drummer ever. Maybe not the best, but the most fun. The smile on his face when he played was like a little kid's. He was *playing* – it was really *play*. He was this great big goofy guy having a blast, and even if he had problems – which I found out later he did, a lot – they didn't exist when he was at his drums.

There was no way I could watch the whole movie. I got so excited, I had to run down to my drums to play, *Play,* not practise. Nobody was home, so I could really go nuts – I didn't have to worry about my mom coming in to complain about the noise or, worse, watch. I was whacking away and going wild, slamming those suckers and yowling my head off: 'I need you . . . *tonight!*' My hair all fell out of my ponytail, sweat was flying. I couldn't care less – I was *rocking*. That whole feeling of finding something cool and real and *mine* came back to me in a stampede.

Before I knew it, it was almost midnight and I hadn't even had dinner. I swear, my stomach was literally rumbling. I went to the kitchen and nuked some Ben & Jerry's Chunky Monkey to soften it. Then I stuck a big spoon in it, pulled out the entire pint's worth and started eating it like a drippy, psychotic popsicle. My thoughts wandered to Stella. That was happening a lot lately. I thought about Stella when I was happy, and I thought about Stella when I was blue, and I thought about her in between too. That night, I wondered what she was up to and how she was feeling and if she was possibly thinking about me. Was she in bed yet? Was she asleep? I wanted to call her and be like, 'Whatever you did I bet it wasn't as fun as my night!'

The Voice

For the first time in my entire life, I had secrets from my mom. That *Dirty Boots* song? Not in a million years could I tell her about it. Gosh, I didn't know how I could possibly sing it. Then Mr Wandweilder explained to me that words are just words – it's how we interpret them that matters. In fact, he said, that's one of the most important things that singers do – bring meaning to lyrics. One person might sing 'Satan's got her tongue' and make it sound like a good thing, but someone else might sing it as a warning.

That made sense to me – sort of. But the truth is, I felt a thrill singing those words. So right there, two secrets: the song, and then the thrill . . . The weekend after our first practice, I bet my mom thought I'd gone clean out of my mind. One minute all I wanted to do was cuddle with her or make waffles, and the next I had my headphones on, giving her one-word answers. I wasn't being sassy, just . . . I didn't want her to know what was ping-ponging in my brain. When she asked about rehearsal I just smiled and said it went real good, that we did a song by Sonic Youth. That seemed to appease her – she must have reckoned it was a nice band since it had the word 'youth' in it. We were supposed to be taking the weekend off, so I tried not to think about the song, or the other kids – but that was hard.

I thought about Wynn – but since she was so nice and didn't put on airs, there wasn't much to think about. Stella was a different story altogether. The way she strutted around, she acted like she was already a star, but she was only the darn bass player – and not even a good one. Wynn wasn't any good at the drums, either, but if she messed up she would blush and say 'sorry.' When Stella messed up, she would not even apologize; she would curse.

Now, A/B could really play. I was so impressed by him. Thinking about A/B gave me a thrill in the same sort of way *Dirty Boots* did. And although to be perfectly honest we sounded like a bunch of barnyard cats, I knew from that first rehearsal that the four of us had . . . something. Only thing I can liken it to is Slapdash Cuckoo Cake. That's what my grandmomma bakes when she's got too much this and not enough that. It's supersweet (since everyone has two full bags of sugar in the cupboard!) and a little flat and usually contains too many nuts, plus the food colouring in the frosting is always off. It really should taste awful but my word to heaven it's one of my favourite treats.

Well, that weekend, Friday night, Saturday night, I could barely sleep. Come Sunday, I had trouble getting up for church. I was awfully grumpy but trying not to act that way, and I couldn't concentrate on the sermon. That made me feel worse. When you're in church you're supposed to be listening to the preacher, you're-supposed to be praying, you're supposed to be thinking about Jesus – not about your problems. Well, I couldn't stop yawning, and then my eyes fluttered shut.

That's when Jesus came to me.

Maybe it was an actual vision. Maybe it was a dream. All I know is Jesus took my hand and we went walking. Then He asked me if I ever went to the movies.

I thought, *You're my personal saviour – don't you know every single thing I do?* But I said, 'Sure – sometimes.'

And Jesus asked if I believed an actress in a movie was the same person as the part that she played.

'Don't be silly, Jesus! Of course not,' I replied. 'No matter how good she is in the movie, she goes home at night, takes off her costume, and settles back into being her.'

That's when Jesus switched up the subject. He asked how it felt when I dropped LuAnn for Kendall. For a minute I just pondered back on that. I was eleven and set to sing that *Titanic* song, *My Heart Will Go On*, in a pageant. A week before the show, I got upset because I knew no matter how well I sang, the song had no meaning for me. No personal meaning. The way it would have if I were singing to a boy, a boy I was in love with and who was in love with me. But I'd never had a boyfriend. The night before the pageant I'd taken a bath, and when I stepped from the tub and caught sight of myself in the mirror, I did not love what I saw. And I was ashamed of those thoughts, ashamed of not loving myself and ashamed of even looking at myself that way.

I went to my mom's room and she wanted to know why I had my lip poked out, but I couldn't explain. Back then I was confused, but as I thought on it for Jesus it became clear that something had gone down the drain with the bathwater. An invisible but very real layer of protection that a child must surrender in order to grow up. What a topsy-turvy feeling it was, like discovering a fresh bruise you're not sure how you got.

My mom was putting the finishing touches on my costume, and when I told her – I mean, asked her if I could just wear the top, a ruffled shirt, with blue jeans instead of the poufy skirt, she began to understand. The skirt was for her baby girl – her baby girl had gone in for a bath, but a different person, someone who could pick her own clothes and preferred blue jeans, had come out. My mom's face went a million ways – from flustered to teary to finally smiley. She accepted that I was growing up, and she agreed. No more poufy skirts. The name change followed naturally later that night. It was more mature, sophisticated. Yes, Kendall Taylor. Presenting Kendall Taylor. Put your hands together for Miss Kendall Taylor.

Going to bed that night, I felt real happy about that, which is basically what I told Jesus. 'Well, Jesus, it felt different, yet very natural,' I said. 'It made me feel like I had . . . developed, *advanced* in some way. I was still me, but there was a new part to me, and the funny thing was the new part felt like it had always been there, waiting for me to discover it.'

Well, Jesus just smiled.

Suddenly, the clouds in my brain began to clear. I asked Jesus if when I sang certain songs another part of me could kind of take over. All at once I recalled what Mr Wandweilder said about finding the voice within the voice. That voice, that girl, was my inner rock star. She could shine like a diamond – and cut like a knife. And she *was* me when I sang *Dirty Boots* or whenever I wanted or needed to be tough, to be cool, to be hot.

Gosh, I felt so happy and relieved and thankful. I guess I must have giggled out loud, because I felt the back of my mom's hand tap against my knee, reminding me I was in church. And when it came time to sing, I poured my joy into those hymns – so much joy everyone at the service could have just floated home on it.

After church my mom took me to the mall. We ate at my favourite place, but while I tore through my steak sandwich and chocolate sundae, she picked at her meal and didn't say much. Next we went to a department store because my mom needed blouses for work – and that's when she started talking a blue streak. She told me that things were getting super-hectic in her office. Because of that, she wouldn't be able to bring me into the city any more for rehearsals. If I wanted to be in this band, I'd have to take the bus, and learn how to get from the Port Authority to the practice space by myself – although Mr Wandweilder would arrange for a car service to take me home.

'So how do you feel about all this, Kendall, honey?' she asked, worry in her voice, a load of blouses in her arms.

I didn't even blink. 'Don't worry, Mom. It will be fine. I'm fifteen. And I really want to be in this band. All my life we've been working for a chance like this.'

My mom hugged me right there in the middle of Macy's, nearly smothering me in polyester. Then she asked if I wanted or needed anything while we were at the mall. 'Shoes,' popped out of my mouth, so we went to Payless. My mom sat on a bench and fussed over her day planner while I roamed the racks. Before long, I picked out the most perfect pair. Shiny, black ankle boots with pointy toes and heels like a pencil. I tried them on. They pinched at the toes and were awfully hard to walk in, but I didn't care. They were just what my inner rock star needed. I went to show my mom – and she burst out laughing. That made my face get hot.

What on earth had come over me, thinking she would buy me such a pair of boots? What on earth had come over me that I would even *want* such a pair of boots? Well, it wasn't like I could tell her. So I stared at the floor – at my feet in those must-have high-heeled boots. My mom told me to go pick out some sensible sneakers or something and be quick about it because she didn't have all day.

I tottered back to the racks, took off the boots, and put on my own shoes. All I could think about was how important it was to get those boots . . . those shiny, pointy, *dirty* boots. So I turned them over to make sure there weren't any security tags on them. Then, very carefully, I slipped them in my bag.

The Boy

They say that breaking up is hard to do. They're wrong.
Breaking up is insane. I've been through it many times
and it doesn't get easier. God, no – not with a girl. With me and
girls, whatever brief, possibly hallucinatory things I had always
sort of petered out on their own. I'm talking about breaking up
with a band. Because that's what I had to do the weekend after
the first 6X rehearsal. Yes, the mandate was to be normal, but
dealing with band stuff is normal for me.

Before I met the girls, I kept playing with Rosemary's
Plankton in a state of utter denial – as if it might somehow go
somewhere. I'd think, *Maybe Bandmate A will actually be ready to
rock instead of dick around. Or maybe Bandmate B will remember to
show up at all. Or wonder of wonder, miracle of miracles, maybe
Bandmate C will have taken his recommended daily Ritalin allowance
and be able to concentrate.* Pipe dreams.

It became excruciatingly clear to me that Rosemary's
Plankton must be stopped after one hookup with Stella,
Kendall, and Wynn. Not because we made zee beautiful music
together – far from it. It was chemical, but not in a science-y
way; please excuse me for lapsing into *Lord of the Rings* mode,

but it was a magic feeling. Yet at the same time it was just plain practical. This gorgeous blonde with a rack on drums – what sleazy record exec could resist? You couldn't buy a better gimmick at the gimmick store.

So I had to be a man and get myself out of Rosemary's Plankton, posthaste. I head over to Bandmate A's house at four o'clock Saturday afternoon like I have for the past year, and we wait for the other two guys to show up, and then they all start bullshitting about bullshit. Inside I'm going *tick-tick-tick* like a time bomb, but I tell myself to be rational, civilized, cool. Finally, Bandmate A or B or C says, 'So what do you wanna work on?' I stand up and it goes down like this:

Me: No.

Bandmate C: Huh?

Me: No. I said 'no.'

Bandmate A: No what? What do you mean 'no'?

Bandmate C: What did he say?

Bandmate B: He said 'no.' But we don't know what he means by 'no.' Don't you wanna practise? You're the one who always says we're not serious enough.

Bandmate A: Yeah. You wanna play X-Box instead?

Me: No. I do not want to play X-Box. And I do not want to practise. I . . . I don't want to be in the band anymore.

Bandmate B: If you don't want to practise, why did you bring your guitar?

Bandmate A: Yeah, if you don't want to be in the band anymore, why did you bring your guitar?

Bandmate C: Are we gonna play X-Box? Cool…

Me: I don't know. I don't know why I brought my guitar. I

guess it's Pavlovian. It's Saturday, it's four o'clock, I bring my guitar. But the reality is I want out of this band.

Bandmate B: How come, man?

Me: Because I wanna *go* somewhere. And Rosemary's Plankton isn't going anywhere.

Bandmate A: What are you talking about? We have a gig!

Me: Your sister's fourteenth birthday party, right here in this very basement, does not count as a gig. Not to me. You guys don't understand. I want to do music. With my *life*. And if I don't start now, and get serious, I'm gonna go to some stupid college and get some stupid job and be miserable and bald before my time.

Bandmate A: So what does that mean? You can't play with us this afternoon? Like you got something better to do?

Me: Yes. No. Look, guys, it was fun and we had a good time but I think I've got something else, finally, that's gonna take off.

Bandmate B: The *chick* band? You've got to be kidding. Dude, girls can't rock out.

Bandmate A: Are you gay? That's it, isn't it? You're gay! A/B's gay.

Bandmate C: He's gay? A/B's gay? Hey, man, that's OK. We don't care if you're gay.

Me: I am not gay. I . . . am . . . a . . . MUSICIAN! Damn it!

Stunned silence all around for about thirty seconds as the profundity of my meaning seeps in.

Bandmate B: So can we keep the name?

Me: Rosemary's Plankton? You still want to be Rosemary's Plankton? That was my name – I came up with that name. How can you be Rosemary's Plankton without me?

Bandmate B: Well, I guess we'll have to find a way, man. Since you're a traitor. Since you're just walking out on what we've all worked so long and so hard at, I say you don't *deserve* the name Rosemary's Plankton.

Me: You know what? You're right. I don't. Be Rosemary's Plankton. You have my blessing.

Bandmate A: OK.

Bandmate B: Cool.

Bandmate C: So are we gonna play X-Box or what?

Bandmate A: I guess.

Bandmate B: Sounds good to me.

Me: I'm in . . .

Later that night, in my room, on my bed, I'm glad that the breakup was relatively painless. A sentimental wave washes over me – *awww, I'll miss those guys* – but it's bullied aside by excitement over the new band . . . and those three babes . . . er, ladies . . . um, women. Then I get the guilts and prod my mind back to Rosemary's Plankton. But all I can think is that Rosemary's Plankton has to be the dumbest name in creation. Suddenly, it occurs to me that we don't have a name for the new combo yet, and I hope I'll have the good sense to just stay out of it. Rosemary's Plankton! Jeeeesus!

The Voice

It sure was smart of Mr Wandweilder to have us weigh real life versus the rock-and-roll life. So much sacrifice comes with a music career. Take PEP! That stands for People, Energy, Power! and it's the pep squad in my school. I was the most spirited member ever, but with meetings and practices and games all year long, well, I had to make a decision. But I'll tell you what, there was really no contest. I chose the band.

We all did. We made a covenant. And nothing made that covenant feel more carved on a marble tablet than the day we took our name.

Gosh, by now I bet everyone's wondering what the heck 6X means. The way we came up with it was very democratic. That's one of the best things about our band: it's a democracy. This is *our* band — not Wynn's band or A/B's band or Stella's band or even my band. Just because one person happens to have more talent, it doesn't matter — we are all equal.

Anyway, we needed a name real bad, so we decided to think some up for our next band meeting. I got in trouble in maths that week — the teacher came around to check our work and I was just doodling ideas in my notebook. The truth is, though,

I couldn't think of any good ones. That bothered me. On one hand I felt: *Shoot, why should I have to name the band – I'm 'The Voice.'* But at the same time I wished I could come up with the best name ever.

Mine were all so silly, I didn't even want to say them. Plus I figured Stella would be on my neck either way – for not saying anything or for saying something dumb. In fact, she was on my neck the minute we got to the Cup 'n' Saucer – that's the coffee shop we go to after practice. We slid into a booth – me and A/B on one side, Stella and Wynn on the other – and all I did to rile her up was open a menu.

Stella reached over and yanked on it. 'Kendall, we've got some decisions to make here that don't have anything to do with "You want fries with that?"'

I closed the menu. But I was pretty hungry, and I poked my lip out.

Stella was like, 'Oh, so we're all pouty now – what, you missed your six o'clock Butterfinger break?' which I ignored, because I am so above that kind of comment. Then she said, 'Look, don't worry. This is gonna be one short meeting because I got our name right here!'

That's when Wynn picked up her menu. 'I am just dying for a tuna melt!' she declared, all breezy and lahdi-dah. The way she ignored Stella – that was unusual. 'Or maybe a BLT,' she went on. 'I haven't had bacon since my stepdad was on Atkins.' A busboy placed four water glasses in front of us, and Wynn turned his way to smile as if he'd just handed her the Miss America bouquet.

Stella twisted in the booth, showing Wynn her pissy face –

mouth stretched out straight and eyes all flashy. 'What's up your ass, Miss Barbie?'

Wynn put her menu down. 'Look, Stella, I'm sorry,' she said. 'It's not that we don't want to discuss band names, but we rocked hard for three hours and are entitled to a sandwich.'

A/B nudged me under the table. 'Here, here!' he said. 'I second the motion from the sandwich coalition!'

I had to giggle at that.

Wynn kept at Stella. 'And then you announce that you have the perfect name, like you don't think we're capable of thinking up some good names too. You think you're going to say your name and we're all going to faint and fall on the floor because it's so brilliant.'

Stella's mouth went from stretched straight to popped open. I bet she was shocked to hear Wynn talking to her all defiant. Before she could come back with a comment, though, the waitress appeared, and we all stared at the woman like she had three heads. Then Wynn ordered her tuna melt, pretty as you please. As for me, well, I didn't have a chance to study the menu so I just asked for a burger deluxe. I don't remember what A/B got, but since Stella was all pissy, she just crossed her arms and ordered coffee.

Then Wynn suggested we go around the table and give our ideas.

'Fine!' said Stella. She slapped her hand on the table, making waves in our water glasses. 'I'll go first. The Hot Shits!'

I couldn't help myself – I let out a hoot. A/B laughed too.

'What, you got a problem with it?' Stella said, scowling.

'Stella,' Wynn said calmly. 'We cannot call our band The Hot Shits.'

'Why not? You want some wussy little cutesy name like . . . like . . . Wynnie and the Pooh-Poohs? We gotta have a name that says we are hot and we know it.'

'Yeah, Stella, but just one problem,' A/B said, tapping a straw from its paper sleeve. 'You can't tell people we're The Hot Shits unless you intend to go up to each and every fan personally and whisper it in their ear.'

'What are you talking about?' she asked.

Glances bounced between the three of us. Stella really didn't get it.

'Stella, "shit" is a swear word,' Wynn said like she was talking to a toddler.

'Yeah . . . and . . . your point?' said Stella.

'Stella, Stella, Stelllaaaah,' howled A/B. 'You can't say "shit" on the radio. You can't print "shit" on your CD.'

Well, her face just fell. She flopped back against the booth, struck dumb. And didn't it tickle me to see her trap shut – even if for only a second! 'Shit,' she said finally. 'So much for freedom of speech.'

A/B blew his straw sleeve at her. Slowly Stella shook her head. 'Oh, now you've done it,' she muttered, dunking fingers in her water glass, pulling out some ice cubes and hurling them at A/B. He shoved against me to duck, the two of us went down in the booth, and there he was, pretty much on top of me, his shaggy hair on me, his laughing breath on me, his face so close I could see spit on his teeth. For one very long second, I didn't know where we were or how we got there. Then I smelled grease – our food had come – and A/B let me up.

Stella went straight for my french fries *and* Wynn's pickle, and I'm sure she helped herself to whatever was on A/B's plate too. 'All right, fine, but look,' she said. 'We gotta have a name that says we're hot shit without using those words exactly.'

A/B went after my french fries too. Why is it that when you sit down with people in New York City they think they have rights to your supper? 'OK, I'll admit it right now,' he said, waving a fry. 'I don't have this big list of band names –'

'Oh, I don't either,' I interrupted, relieved.

'But I like the hot-shit message idea,' he continued. 'We need a name we can imagine millions of people bellowing at the top of their lungs.'

'We could call ourselves The Greatest,' I offered.

'Excuse me, but have you ever even heard of Mohammed Ali?' Stella said before it was even all out my mouth.

Talk about riding a turtle to nowhere. Every name one of us came up with, somebody else had a reason to shoot it down. Soon we were done eating and the waitress brought our bill. Then I said, 'Well, if we want to be rich and famous, why don't we call ourselves Success?'

Stella snickered in that Stella way. 'Maybe because Success sucks ass?'

After a moment, this expression of pure glory came over Wynn's face. She went, 'Ohhhh!' almost like a whisper, but it made us look her way. She'd been awfully quiet since sniping with Stella earlier. Plus, I think she probably had a big old list of names in that journal she always carries, and she probably expected that we'd all have a list too, but once things took off in this free-for-all way, she just kept mum, chewing her tuna melt, the journal beside her in the booth. But the smile she got right then was so big and beamy, we all noticed.

'You guys,' she said, 'remember when you were little – um, not you A/B, sorry – and you actually began to realize you were a girl, that you were different from boys? All of a sudden you cared about things like what clothes you wore, what colour they were . . . ?'

'Did you leap into some kind of parallel universe?' Stella asked, snapping her fingers at Wynn. 'Because clearly you have no idea as to what this conversation over here is about –'

'No, I do, I swear. Just think – do you remember?'

'What, being a little kid? Shit, yes, I have full retention of my faculties. What does that have to do with anything?'

Wynn was so eager she looked like a child herself. 'Your mother takes you to the store to buy some outfits, and it *matters* to you, because you know you're a girl, and that's crucial.'

Although I had no idea where she was headed, I got caught up in what Wynn was going on about. 'Yes,' I told her. 'It's like a tiny epiphany.' Stella still had her stubborn face on, like even if she got what Wynn meant she wouldn't admit it. And I'll tell you what, I liked that fine – Wynn and Kendall instead of Wynn and Stella for a change.

Wynn reached across the table and took my hand. 'See? Kendall knows – that on-the-verge feeling, that first-taste feeling.'

'That's right!' I said. 'That's exactly it.'

'OK,' Wynn squeezed my hand. 'So . . . what size do you wear?'

I felt my hand go clammy. 'What size . . . ? You mean, in clothes?'

'Yes! What size is that cute little outfit?'

'I – I don't know . . . I don't remember . . .' Right then, I felt like I'd just dropped my ice-cream cone in the dirt.

Then Stella slapped the table. 'I know!' she hollered, like the epiphany just caught up with her. 'I know . . . 6X.'

And Wynn shrieked. She let go of my hand and threw both of hers in the air.

'What?' I asked.

'Huh?' said A/B, who was even more baffled.

Wynn started bouncing up and down in the booth. '6X! Yes! Yes!'

Then Stella got to bouncing up and down too. 'Girl, you are a freakin' genius!'

Well, Wynn and Stella were bouncing and while they were bouncing they started hugging and laughing till they were almost crying. Then Stella turned towards us. 'Oh God! Look at you two!' she wailed. Then back to Wynn: 'Look at them!'

Wynn took a napkin to wipe at her eyes. 'Oh God,' she said. 'Stella – can you explain?'

'Wait, wait – let me calm down a sec.' She pushed dramatically at her Afro a couple of times, made the sound of 'phew.' Then she said. 'All right, it's like this – it's *symbolic*. 6X, it's a turning point. It's a size thing, the first size of clothing you actually make a choice over, it's a symbol of not being a baby any more, you're . . . something else, you're female, you're *conscious,* and you're on your way.'

'Ohhhh . . .' I got it then — and it was absolutely beautiful to me.

'But wait — there's more,' Wynn went on. 'The idea came to me because of what Kendall said about success. It's word play: Success . . . 6X?'

'Ohhhh . . .' It was doubly beautiful, it really, really was. 'It's perfect,' I said.

Then it was all eyes on A/B. Our boy. Would he — could he — possibly understand? Because he *had* to. He poked at the melting ice in his glass with his straw. Then he said, '6X . . . ike success, yep, I get that.' He sucked at his watery Coke. 'And it's also some girl-power trip — OK, that's cool.' Then he gave us a look like a villain in a cartoon. 'But to me, 6X — something about it,' he said. 'It kind of also sounds like . . . sex.'

The Boss

6X has it all. Short and easy to remember? Check. All about chick power? Check. But you don't get the meaning straight off, so it's not corny – it's cryptic, and that makes people curious. Plus, it has double meaning for us as a takeoff on success. And goddamn if every guy doesn't think it implies sex. Even Brian, the second he heard it – typical guy reaction: '6X, I like it, I like it a lot,' he said. 'It sounds like sex.' Cool with me: Sex sells.

That's the thing I love about Brian: For all his passion for the art part, he is the same as me about the bottom line. The marketability factor. The business side. Our band is a product just as much as it's a creation, and once the product had a name we were ready to kick it to the next level.

For the next few months, we practised our asses off. Once we had *Dirty Boots* and *You're All I've Got Tonight* down, we got to learn the Tom Petty and the GBV songs. Brian started bringing guests into the studio when we rehearsed. He had Alan Slushinger, the guy from Windows by Gina – you know that band? He's the main songwriter and bass player, but he's also this producer who's done some very cool records. And O, the guy who basically *is* The Oms, he came in too. These are Brian's boys, who he runs with. They'd give us pointers; sometimes even sit in – that's industry-talk for play with us. But I don't believe it was all casual. See, Brian's always planning. Even at that stage of the game I think he was checking out potential producers and extra players for our album.

He also had this lady named Denni or Danni Something come by. She was annoying because someone forgot to tell her she was too old to dress like a teenager. But she's important so I was cool to her. She does this Internet industry newsletter that everyone who's anyone reads. So that's the calibre of people we were meeting – and by then we were sounding so good, I wasn't even nervous playing in front of them.

The fact that I could hang with these people no problem really impressed Brian. I could tell – there were all these tiny cues, smiles, and nods he would give me, body language. And then the time Alan Slushinger sat in, I was leaving the bathroom and saw him with Brian, saying good-bye at the elevator, so I went over too. I thanked Alan for showing me how to do these bass chords, then joked that I hoped I never had to actually play anything that difficult. Alan agreed, and we all laughed. Once he bounced, Brian gave me this look I can't exactly describe – admiring, but a little amused. I let him look at me all he wanted; I liked how it made me feel – though I can't describe that exactly either. 'So what do you say?' he said eventually. 'Will success change Stella Saunders?'

I knew what he meant . . . Look, don't put this in the final cut, but I was trying to drag out the moment, because Brian and I hardly have any damn alone time. So I stood there, pretending to contemplate the question as the elevator cranked out its asthmatic blues. Brian put his arm up against the wall and leaned on it, making a shield with his body. I like that he's just tall enough for me to have to tilt my head to look in his eyes – taller than me, but not too tall. From that angle, in that light, I saw a shadow of stubble along his jaw and above his lip, a shade or two sandier than the hair on his head. His beard looked soft, almost furry – not like the bristle my dad gets when he needs a shave. Finally I said, 'What do you mean, change me?'

Brian grinned. 'Well, right now you're so *into* everything – cool, not gaga, but avid, eager. You're like a sponge,' he said, his face getting more serious as he spoke. 'But will you be different when the red carpet starts rolling? Will fame take away your enthusiasm? Will it make you too hot to handle?' He grinned again. 'You know, turn you into an asshole?'

I shook my hair out and looked up at him. 'Come on, Brian,' I said. 'Be real. I could never be an asshole.' Then I thrust out my hip for a dose of attitude. 'And I'm already too hot too handle.'

Just as I was giving him a chance to let my last remark sink in, A/B came bounding out of our practice room like some happy, yappy mutt, rhapsodizing about how much he loved Windows by Gina and how awesome it was to have Alan Slushinger sit in – he was lucky he didn't wet himself. So much for respecting two people in an intimate moment.

Whatever. The next step for the band was to do a showcase. That's a gig you play for the industry – record company people, radio people, journalists, and shit. It's one way you start a buzz. And if someone from a record company likes you – bam, you could get signed on the spot. Knowing we were gonna do a showcase really juiced us up. It was like: *All right, now we have a real goal*. The showcase would go down in about a month. The specifics were in Gaylord's court. He'd try to have us play the Mercury Lounge or CBGB. The funny thing is, none of us are even old enough to get into a club on the regular, but here we'd be playing at one – we joked about that.

With the showcase on the way, our rehearsal schedule would be kicked into overdrive, so Brian got me to enroll in this program at school called Flex-Learn – it lets you accelerate in the subjects you're good in so you can basically keep it moving, even graduate sooner.

Wynn and I are both in Flex-Learn, but she's not in as many FL classes as me. See, Wynn, if she doesn't happen to naturally do well in a subject, her way is to just coast. She doesn't care if she gets a C or an A. Me, I strive. For one thing I'm not rich, so I don't have it in the back of my mind that I'll always be taken care of. But I'm also just competitive by nature. Plus I definitely intend to graduate high school as soon as possible, for one very obvious reason: rock stardom.

The Boy

Oh yeah, I was psyched. A bona fide showcase – that was the kind of gig I've dreamed about my entire life. I figured I'd get stage fright the night of, but thinking about it, practising for it, I was cool. There was, however, something weighing heavy on my mind – a hurdle to leap, a river to forge: the dreaded party with the parents. Say it with me now: 'Oy vey.'

Wandweilder was high on the notion that we have this dinner in a nice restaurant: him, us, and all our parents. It was essential, he said, that our progenitors feel included in the band. Give them an inch of involvement and we'll save a mile of meddling – that was his theory. He also explained that parents have this burning need to meet others of their ilk. They decide whether they want their kids to hang out with other kids by their parents – what they do for a living, where they went to college, whether they prefer a Chardonnay to a Chenin Blanc. After this dinner, the parents would know we were OK by seeing how respectable our parents are. Plus, they would bond over stuff like property taxes and high cholesterol.

Brian has a way of making even the most insane things sound reasonable.

Honestly, though, the thing I was freaked out about had nothing to do with parents. As you can plainly see, I'm an NJB: a nice Jewish boy. I'm reasonably intelligent and polite – conversant in Parentese. And I clean up OK. Nope, my issue had to do with the other three quarters of 6X. So far, my interaction with my bandmates had been purely professional. Even the post-practice coffee-shop hangs were career-related – rehearsal wind-downs, if you will. But this party would be social. The girls would dress up. Cleavage would quite possibly be on display. Perfume would most certainly be in the air.

This was a problem since I already harboured an infinitesimal crush on each bandmate, and I was trying to keep that under control. Wynn – beyond the body is this softness, this sweetness, this *soul*. Kendall – that optimistic, clueless thing she's got going on, it's really cute. And in contrast is Stella, the wild woman. I figured she had the most experience, so if I were to lose my virginity to her –

Oh, shit, tell me I did not just let that slip. Can I take it back? Let's leave that little tidbit on the cutting room floor, please.

The point is, thus far my little lustings were in check, but if they were placed in the petri dish of a social situation, who knew what might grow? So I was sweating.

The restaurant was in Little Italy, the kind of family-style place where you don't even order, they just keep bringing out massive platters piled with food. Although it wasn't fancy, the girls, as I feared, definitely went the extra mile in the primp department. Kendall had a skirt on – not too short, but I saw her knees. Unlike the girls at my school – Lawrence, Long Island, being Bulimia Central – Kendall has meat on her bones, which is nice, and that night I noticed she has dimples on her knees, the kind of dimples you want to squeeze to see if that will make her jump. Stella was my rock 'n roll dream: miniskirt, studded belt, black lace-up shit-kickers. A coal mine of smoky eye-makeup. 'Fro parted down the middle into two big pom-poms – made her head look like a boom box with Nerf speakers. Wynn kept it low-key as usual, but I still felt like I was sharing lasagna with a supermodel.

I actually had sympathy for the parents. They were strangers to each other, so that had to suck. Please, I thought, get some booze into these forty-somethings before they implode. My dad led the way: Stoli martini, straight up. The other parents followed suit, except Kendall's mom, who looked like she needed a drink the most. As a widow, she was flying solo. But it didn't take much prodding to get her talking about Kendall's war hero dad – an incredible athlete, active in church, working full-time and in college, who joined the Reserves, got called up . . . and came back in a box. Everyone got pretty misty-eyed after that story.

I can't say the parents bonded, though. My mom and dad must have felt like sharecroppers next to the Shermans. And the Saunders, Stella's parents: I got the impression they were vying to be voted official poster couple for interracial marriage – they're very politically correct. But it seemed to be going OK . . . until the fourth or fifth course, when Mrs Sherman loudly inquired if there was anything in the kitchen that wasn't 'oozing olive oil or dripping red sauce.' Mrs Saunders – whose ancestry originated somewhere between Sicily and Naples, where olive oil and red sauce flow like, well, olive oil and red sauce – marvelled aloud about how a grown woman can exist on a diet of dehydrated celery stalks. Whereas my mother prefers more passive-agressive warfare, these two exchanged glares like stags in a horn-lock. Talk about a non-Kodak moment.

A perfect opportunity for me to excuse myself and slip out for a toke. Surveying the Little Italy scene, joint cupped in my palm, I cooled my heels. A boisterous party of eight tried to decide if they should go to Soho for more drinks; out-of-towners in parkas and bum-bags ambled along the sidewalk, scrutinizing menus. I moved to a more secluded cobblestone street, and just as I was about to light up, a throaty female voice came up behind me.

'What you got there, boy?'

Please-don't-be-a-lady-cop! my brain begged, erotically charged and scared shitless at the same time. *Please-don't-be-a-lady-cop!* Composing my most apologetic rube-from-Long-Island grin, I turned around.

'Psyche!' cried Stella in her own tones. 'Pffff, you thought you were so busted.'

Stella grabbed my sleeve and pulled me into the deserted doorway of a cheese shop, closed for the evening – an ideal smoke spot. It was freezing as we stood together, a foot apart, our breath visible puffs. We hadn't been in such close proximity before and I hoped I wasn't too obvious as I absorbed the full effect of her wide eyes and caramel skin, the way she smelled – not girly or perfumed, but very, very *female*.

'Come on,' she said impatiently. 'Fire it up.'

Several flicks of the Bic later I managed a hit and passed the joint. Stella tried to inhale but I must have rolled it too tight. Giving me a hard look, she spun the butt end between her thumb and index finger a few times to loosen it up. She took a hit, leaned against the doorjamb, and on the exhale told me, 'Your mom's smart – she stayed out of the line of fire when all the other parents were jockeying for position.'

'Oh . . . thanks,' I said and, incapable of finding a follow-up comment, took another toke.

Stella accepted the joint again, gesticulating with it. 'Me, I'm exactly like my mom – always got to get into it. Damn, you sure do roll a pin, A/B. Come on, gimme a shotgun.'

'Huh?' the densest boy in America wondered.

Stella sucked her teeth. 'Please, what kind of pothead are you, you don't know how to give a shotgun? Allow me to school you...' she said, clearly relishing the chance to show off.

She inhaled a long hit, shook the tip of the joint to clear it of ash, and, to my shock and awe, stuck the lit end between her lips. Then, with her free hand, she grabbed my face, squeezing my cheeks till my mouth popped open. Drawing me to her till we were kiss close, she blew hard. A stream of smoke like a rocket's tail spewed from the unlit end of the burning weed, straight into my mouth, a dizzying dose, a double hit that literally knocked me back. My head swam as Stella expertly removed the lit end from her mouth and smiled straight into my eyes. The great big shotgun buzz moved deliciously up through my brain and down through my body, but I wasn't sure how much of what I was feeling had to do with marijuana and how much of it was Stella Saunders.

Apparently, my expression pleased her. She cocked her

82

head approvingly. 'All right,' she said, handing me the joint and arranging herself comfortably against the door. 'Now you do me.'

The Body

Musically, everything was coming together. Brian would record random practices and play them back for us, and more and more I could listen without cringing. Even *You're All I've Got . . .* with me singing. Plus, we had a name we loved, a showcase coming up, our parents were proud of us . . .

And yet . . . I don't know. Do I always have to stress about something? The relationships in the band began to obsess me. Like Stella being catty to Kendall. It made no sense. We need Kendall, so why deliberately upset her? But who was I to call Stella off?

Not that there isn't something odd about Kendall. Your first impression is of this sweet, naïve Southern girl, but she's got a weird streak and it gets wider by the day. Sometimes she'll stop singing in the middle of a song and won't say 'I have to pee' or anything, she'll just leave the room for ten minutes. And the boots thing. Every girl is entitled to her own taste but I'm sorry, those boots are hideous. Plus, it's as if she *smuggles* them in; she comes to practice in sneakers then changes into these ... hooker boots. Unless she's got them on, though, she won't sing a note.

I thought about this a lot. Maybe Kendall feels pressure to be good and pure and Christian, and now she's got this whole rock band thing heaped on her, so what if the two concepts are just snarling her up inside? If it's hard for her, she never says anything to us. In fact, although she's always technically pleasant, sometimes there's this hint of, I don't know, moral superiority or something.

But get her next to A/B and she's another person completely. Her crush must weigh two tons. It's so obvious; Stella will snicker to me about it or roll her eyes, but I refuse to go there. I'm not going to bond with Stella about how Kendall's deluding herself over A/B. Besides, it's not that A/B is leading Kendall on, it's just that he's so nice – I worry she'll take his niceness the wrong way and wind up hurt. But I don't know; maybe A/B *does* have feelings for Kendall . . . or Stella . . . or me – it's hard to tell.

So this was a stressful period. There was no one I could talk to, because I was eating, sleeping, breathing 6X – and everything that was churning me up had to do with those guys. That's why I turned to my journal, I guess. I started writing a lot. Not about how anxious I was – that would only have made me more of a wreck. Mostly I wrote my imaginings, stuff to take me away from reality. Escapism, release, I don't know. I carried my journal everywhere, like a security blanket.

Then something happened. My poems began to morph into songs. Maybe because beat and rhythm were becoming second nature to me, but everything that streamed out of me felt like lyrics. It was completely organic. It's not like I'd ever show my songs to the band. They just . . . gushed. Sometimes I'd get a title in my head out of nowhere – *Hello Kitty Creeps Me Out* is one. I'd have the title and – gush: song. Or I'd be watching TV and one of the characters would inspire me: *All Over Oliver* is about this guy in a soap opera. Then I wrote this one called *Put This in Your Purse (Ashley)* that came out of a conversation I overheard in a bookstore. This girl, Ashley, was telling her friend about how her grandmother makes her steal packets of Sweet 'n' Low from restaurants, even though she's rich enough to *own* Sweet 'n' Low. I just thought that was hilarious and . . . gush: song.

After a while, though, the silly songs started to segue into stuff that actually meant something to me. When that happened, I would slam my journal shut. I was trying to get away from my emotions, not wrestle them onto paper. Not to be too much of a freak or come off possessed, but no matter how hard I tried not to, I *had* to write them. It was as if the songs *made* me write them, if that makes any sense. Those meaningful songs – *(I Am Not a) Lingerie Model* and *My Real Dad Lives in Prague* – they didn't gush, though. They more like leaked. And I let them. There just didn't seem to be anything I could do to make them stop.

The Boy

I could live to be a dinosaur, I could have double-jointed lap dancers written into my touring rider, but I'll never experience anything as crazy as our Stunt Club showcase. It was a roller-coaster ride, all right, with ups and downs, thrills and chills . . . and puke.

And to think I didn't expect much. After all, at that point we were just a cover band – a cool-as-shit cover band, but a cover band nonetheless. Call me a cockeyed pessimist, but if one schmuck who worked in the mail-room at a label like Sony or Universe thought we were the best thing since Cheez Doodles, I'd have gone home happy.

Thanks to Stella, however, there was a decent chance we'd draw a crowd. 'I don't wanna take any chances,' she'd said at our Saturday band meeting, pulling out a sheaf of flyers. 'What we do is, we go down to Union Square and St. Marks Place and anyplace else kids congregate, and hand these suckers out.'

Nobody balked – we didn't have anything better to do – so we hit the streets to paper the city. Stella coerced Wynn into a little flirtatious flyer-passing. 'Those boobs of yours are an insurance policy,' she told her. 'No dude remotely close to puberty will skip a chance to see you and your two friends.'

Wynn visibly squirmed. 'Stella, you are trying to pimp me!'

But Stella linked her arm through Wynn's and insisted with eyelash-fluttering sincerity, 'I am not; I would never do that!' Then she laughed. 'I am trying to pimp 6X! So c'mon, work it a little.'

Wynn sighed, then tossed her hair and blew a kiss. 'How's that?' she asked.

'Perfect!' Stella said. She then deployed us while she supervised from strategic park benches and lampposts. Still, after we'd distributed the lot and convened for sustenance at Farrah's Falafel, she continued cracking the whip. 'These are for later,' she said, handing us each a fat stack of different flyers. 'Friday morning, slip them into every single locker at your school. Wynn and I will do the same.'

I glanced down at the straight-outta-Kinko's paper in front of me: 'Lucien Vickers will be at Stunt Club tonight at 10 PM Will you?'

Kendall's eyes went as large as two vinyl 45s. 'Lucien Vickers will be at the show?' she said.

Stella flashed a triumphant – and not particularly charitable – grin. 'Of course not. But since every girl would gnaw off her right arm to be in a room with him, it won't hurt to make people *think* he will.'

It was brilliant. Hey, even I know Lucien Vickers, lead singer for emo heartthrobs Churnsway. I don't know a single chick that doesn't melt at the mention of his name, and much as it pains me to say so, regular dudes, myself included, like Churnsway.

Kendall wrinkled her nose a bit, but Wynn and I stared at Stella, radiating respect.

Nothing like a little false advertising to help a band go far!

Gig day, I was in robot mode – I just functioned. After school, I went home and put on my 'outfit.' Come on, it's a chick band so you *know* wardrobe was discussed in advance. And loath as I am to admit it, image *is* important. The concept was to keep it simple but still look like a unit: everyone in jeans and some kind of tight shirt, either red or black. Sounds simple enough – but three band meetings and countless telephone calls were devoted to this fashion formula. I can't even remember how we settled on the colours, but the tight-shirt thing was deemed crucial to the 6X ethos, a visual to represent 'bursting out into girlhood.' Hot chicks in tight tops – who am I to argue? I pulled on an ancient summer-camp T-shirt I'd been keeping as a souvenir, doubled up on the deodorant, and headed to the city.

We all hooked up at the Cup 'n Saucer for the ceremonial pre-gig meal. No girly stereotypes there – these ladies ate like starving hyenas. Then we hit the practice space – Gaylord was there to help load our gear into two taxicabs for the ride downtown. I was a little disappointed that we weren't making our debut at the venerable CBGB, but Stunt Club was a hot new place. Plus, we'd be opening for Tiger Pimp, this over-the-top Lower East Side metal act. No one really knows if what they do is parody or homage, which is the main reason they're so popular with a certain hipster element. Gaylord worships them; he'd already seen them five times.

Just as we were starting our sound check, Tiger Pimp stomped into Stunt wearing full eighties regalia. Platform shoes, flowing scarves, shiny skintight pants – the whole nine. It must have messed with our confidence because we sucked a wet moose at sound check. Four bars into our first song, *boing!* – I broke a string. Then, the Tiger Pimp drummer (I still don't know if it's a he or a she) started giving Wynn the evil eye, which threw her off. Worst of all was Kendall – her voice was shaky. (Nerves? The fact that she hadn't performed her sneakers-to-high-heels ritual yet? Who knew?) We elected to cut our test run short.

Compared to the places I'd played before, Stunt was massive. Plus, it was like the English muffin of rock clubs, lots of nooks and crannies. We found an area to hole up and sulk in. Stella drank four Red Bulls in rapid succession, which got her all amped. She paced and grimaced, reminding me of this female prison movie I caught on Cinemax late one night. Wynn was quiet, staring off into space, occasionally jotting notes in her journal. Kendall disappeared for half an hour, and when she returned (from the ladies' room, I presume) she had all her make-up on. Not that I'm one to judge this kind of thing, but I mean she had *all* her makeup on.

'How do I look?' she asked.

'Nice!' Wynn said quickly, shooting Stella a pleading 'don't start' face. 'You look nice.'

Stella threw up her hands. 'Yeah,' she said. 'Real nice.'

'Real nice,' I parroted.

'It's just . . . a little beauty pageant-y,' Wynn went on carefully.

'Is that bad?' Kendall asked. 'I *will* be the centre of attention, after all.'

'No, yes – it's not bad; you do have to shine,' Wynn told her. 'Just maybe . . . just . . . if we could take it down a notch?'

Kendall plunked herself on a chair, letting Wynn wipe half a pound of pink gunk off her face. Around that time, our parents started showing up. They didn't go overboard with the *kvelling*, though – just said hello before heading off to find 'good seats.' Still, the presence of parents spooked Stella, who insisted we go backstage and practise our moves one more time. We'd decided that a few traditional rock star moves would make our show a show – not a bunch of stiffs standing around playing instruments. So I taught Stella the midair jump-and-split while I took the windmill whack for myself. Kendall was working on a mike stand kick-twirl, and even though she didn't quite have it down, it was cute the way she did it – clumsy-cute. Wynn was the only one without a move. She didn't want one. We were all cool with that. None of us doubted that Wynn would have all eyes on her.

And she did. Just not in the way any of us could have ever predicted.

The Boss

Brian poked his head backstage and just said, 'OK, guys – let's do this.' And simple as that we filed out onto the stage. No introduction – that would have been corny. The place was packed, and I take full credit for that. Why leave it up to fate when you can force flyers onto every halfway cool kid in New York, plus parts of New Jersey and Long Island? Yet while I could feel the crowd, I couldn't raise my eyes. The truth is, I was terrified, all right; serious stage fright. My body felt wobbly; my breath came in little puffs – hoo-hoo, hoo-hoo – like some kind of deranged owl. Four words floated around my brain like Alpha-Bits: 'this' 'can't' 'do' 'I.' I had to make sure they didn't link up into 'I can't do this' – or it would come true.

As if I weren't having enough trouble taking care of my own shit – pick up bass, slip strap over head – a sudden punch of panic hit me straight in the gut. Frantic, I glanced left to check that crazy-ass Kendall had changed into her singing boots. Yes! Relief! Seeing those boots, I knew everything would be all right. Behind me, Wynn got the party started with a *click-click* count off. A/B's Dan Electro rang out and my fingers hit notes – the right notes. I could lift my head. Leaning back a step, I looked at Wynn. We matched smiles. Finally, I looked out at the audience. Brian had warned us that usually, at an industry show, people just stand there, too cool to act like they're into you. But there was a sea of nodding heads, some full body wiggling, a fledgling mosh pit forming. I hoped the label suits would be impressed. My smile got shark-sized, like I could eat every person in the house, and I knew I was exactly where I was meant to be.

We finished *The Waiting* and the audience went nuts – applause, hollers, whistles, and 'whoos!' The reaction was so huge, I understood the whole 'feed off the crowd' thing. That enthusiasm is lifeblood, it's nourishment, it's mass love. I scanned the crowd for Brian, but it was impossible to pick anyone out, the way the lights glare back at you.

Once the audience simmered down, Kendall took a little bow. 'Thank you,' she said brightly, adding, 'we sure do love it when you jump around!' which made the crowd roar back at her. But as we surged with the opening of *Dirty Boots* she went into freak mode, closing her eyes and taking these awkward little stagger steps back and forth. That pissed me off big-time: Here she was, improvising a new move – with her eyes shut. What if she fell off the freakin' stage? Kendall's no Beyoncé, all right; she can barely walk in stilettos, much less dance. Yet somehow it suited the mood of the song.

So we're blasting through the set, loud and loose, no problem, no screwups. It's all good. When I go into my half-split, A/B turns to give me the KISS tongue. Wynn sings *You're All I've Got Tonight*, in that murmury semi-flat monotone of hers, a cool indie contrast to Kendall's virtuosity. Part of me

93

doesn't want the set to end, but when you only have four damn songs in your repertoire you wind up pretty quick. We go into *Teenage FBI* ... and talk about a grand finale. What happens next will go down forever in 6X history. It lasts maybe five seconds, but it's monumental. We refer to it now, on those rare times we bring it up, as the Wynn Move.

Kendall doesn't catch it and neither does A/B, since they face the audience pretty much the whole time when we play. But my stance is sort of sideways, half turned to the crowd, half turned to Wynn – that's how we work our bassist-drummer vibe – so I see it all. Me and the entire Stunt Club crowd. During the chorus, Wynn's bopping away, doing that seated pogo thing she does. And then – out it pops. Her boob. The left one. In all it's Double-D glory.

For a split second, I lose it myself. My hands fly off my bass, up to my mouth: 'Holy shit!' What's she gonna do? Keep pounding with her boob flapping? Dash from the stage, crying hysterically?

Well, the rock gods are with her for sure, because what she does is abso-freakin'-lutely inspired. Flip, flip – she tosses her sticks up way over her head. Tumble, tumble, down they come, end over end. As they fall, Wynn yanks at her top, letting Lefty slide back into place with just enough time to catch her sticks and wrap up the song.

The lights go out.

The crowd goes bananas, berserk, ape-shit insane.

I rush toward Wynn, my bass still on – somehow I remember to pull the cable out. She grabs my hand and we rush backstage. The girl is sixteen different shades of blush, but when she looks in my eyes, she cracks up. We start hugging, my bass poking us both, as A/B and Kendall, still completely clueless, race in, whooping and high-fiving.

'Did everyone see?' Wynn asks.

'Whatever, girl, who cares – we were great!' I tell her. 'What, you think all that screaming and clapping is for your left titty?'

'We were, we were – weren't we,' she says. 'We were good!'

'We were *great!*' I repeat, and she clings to me until the parental platoon piles in – Wynn's mother leading the charge.

'Wynn, darling, are you all right?' her mom asks, pinched and tense. I see Wynn gasp for breath and nod up and down, just as my parents swarm all over me. Irritating as this is, I'm chill, I endure it – I know it's coming from a place of pride. Plus, the whole time I'm thinking, *Brian . . . where's Brian?*

I actually start to get upset: *How can he not be here? What is he doing?* I look around. Wynn has put on a sweater and buttoned it up to the neck even though it's boiling backstage. A/B's parents seem pretty calm – they're used to having the most talented kid in the room. Kendall's mom is all stiff in the shoulders and wearing a prim, plastic smile. Gaylord comes in. Alan from Windows by Gina says hi. Complete strangers are pushing their way back just to get a whiff of our just-brought-the-house-down stank. Of course, blab about Wynn's boob circulates like a virus – 'Did you see?' 'Damn, I missed it!' 'The music editor for *Maxim* will be kicking himself for not showing up!' – but my inner publicist knows that can't hurt us. Everybody's smiling. I'm smiling too. I'm also inching toward internal freak-out, ready to scream, 'WHERE IS BRIAN GODDAMN WANDWEILER, DAMN IT?!' when in he struts looking like the canary who ate the cat. I wanna rush over and hug him but once he's here I'm also mad so I just cross my arms and try to look blank while he tells us how awesome we were. Then he asks for everyone but the band members to leave.

'Guys, I have to tell you something, and you're not going to believe it because I don't believe it,' Brian says. His glasses slip down his nose, and he pushes them back up – it's a Brian thing. 'But I just had a tête-à-tête with the head of A&R at Flaxxön Records – and he wants to sign you.'

He's right. We don't believe him. We are so punked. We just stare at him.

'Earth to 6X!' he says, and starts laughing. 'Look, he *gets* it. He's gaga. He wants you. He wants you bad.'

The Body

You know when the girl in the horror movie is walking down the stairs to the basement, probably without a flashlight, probably in her underwear. And you're watching the movie, thinking, no, no, no; bad idea; don't do that; don't go into the basement. You wonder why she's going down there when she's pretty certain something terrible will happen. You think, Oh, I would never go into that basement.

But I think you would.

Here's why: There's this thing in your stomach, this hibernating lump that wakes up at the first sniff of fear. Soon as that kicks in, something else, a buzzy little bug, starts up somewhere around your left ear and goes, 'Oh, really? I shouldn't? Then I *will*.' It's not that you're cocky or think you're invulnerable. You just need to find out exactly what is waiting for you. Terrible, yes, but terrible how? What kind of terrible? Specifically. You can't breathe until you know – even if it will be your last breath. Basically, you *have* to go into that basement.

Only sometimes it's not a basement. Sometimes it's the balcony of a murky club.

Wait, I'm sorry – it's hard to talk about this. But I want to, I et me start from the beginning so I don't seem like a e lunatic . . .

ate. Tiger Pimp have finished their set but I have no idea what time it is, because from the minute I walked into Stunt, time has been doing this crazy thing – slow, fast, seconds take hours and hours fly by, very weird. I'm trying to process everything. My mom and stepdad are there, Brian, all the guys. A bunch of people I don't know. Everyone's . . . crackling. Adrenaline rushing but trying to relax. Ambient music floats around us like smoke. We're sitting at these tables, everyone chattering at once. Brian's halfway out of his seat, telling a story; my mom is sitting next to him, her hand on his arm. Someone orders champagne and everyone except Kendall and Mrs Taylor indulges.

That's when Dylan Stop – wait, oh my God, I can't believe I almost blurted out his whole name. That *has* to be cut or there'll be all kinds of lawsuits. And the name of the record company too. But this will be edited for our protection, so I can say it. Right this second, as I'm telling this, I *want* to say it; I want to hear it come out of my mouth: Dylan Stoppard. Dylan Stoppard. The man who wants to sign 6X. He's sitting opposite me, crooking his index finger. Once he realizes I notice this, he looks all happy, but in a lazy way – like he just got a present he'd always wanted, but it wasn't a surprise. Very slightly, very slowly, he leans towards me – and I do the same, slightly, slowly. Then our faces are close, and he whispers, 'Wynn, would you like to do a bump?'

After that, we have a whole conversation in tiny gestures. I sit back in my seat and glance around; everyone's oblivious to us. My mom and stepdad seem to be getting into a tiff. Stella is standing on her knees on her chair; she's pounding her chest with her fist. Nobody's paying attention to me except for Dylan Stoppard. And I am returning the favour. Not because of what he looks like – casual tan, crooked nose, buzzed hair, and deep black eyes like twin tar pits – but because of how he looks, bored and intense at the same time, and supremely confident. The sort of person who'd be at ease anywhere – a frat house, a crack house, the White House. And oh, he's cagey. The way his head's tilted down, he could be examining his fingernails, but we both know he's examining me.

Then he juts out his chin, to mean, *Well? Do you or don't you?* I stare at him, unblinking, trying to psyche him out, but he gives me these bug eyes and I start to crack. I look away, look back. He's smirking. I shrug. He puts up his hand, stop-sign-style, the signal for 'Wait.' Then, purposefully, he lets his eyes travel around the club; I follow his eyes with mine – the stairs, a balcony. Then he gets up and walks away. I wait. I sip some champagne. Count to fifteen, twenty, twenty-five, thirty. Now it's my turn.

I'm not going for the drugs. I don't even know what a 'bump' is but I figure it's some drug reference. The bump is the excuse, the bait. Dylan Stoppard knows that. I know it too. I'm going because he wants me to. What I want? Sorry, I don't even think about that. Not once. Not at all. It's not even an issue. Up in the balcony, I find him on a sofa in the corner. He seems very comfortable. If he were an animal, he'd be some kind of mutant cross between a cat and a bear. I don't sit down next to him, and he doesn't ask me to.

'I lied,' he says.

He speaks very quietly, I can barely hear him, but I still don't want to sit next to him so I sit on the table in front of him. He blends into the darkness; his dark suit, his wavy dark hair, the prickly dark stubble on his face. He doesn't smell of cologne, but there must be a cigar in his jacket pocket – he smells of that, and something else I can't identify, something dark and thick.

'What did you say?' I ask.

'I lied,' he repeats. 'I don't have any coke.'

'Oh, is that what a bump is?' I say casually. 'I don't care. I don't really do drugs.'

'Yeah,' he says. 'Neither do I.' Then he sips his cognac. 'You don't want to sit next to me.'

It's a statement, not a question, so I don't answer. In fact, I don't think I say another word to him. Dylan Stoppard does the talking in that quiet, lulling voice. I try to place his accent, but he doesn't have one – he speaks like he doesn't come from anywhere. And he speaks sparingly; he does not waste words, he selects them, like he's buying fruit, or a cashmere scarf.

'That's fine,' he says. 'I like you where you are right now. I can see you.'

Dylan Stoppard is attempting to seduce me. And he's doing it in this very pure way. By 'pure' I mean he doesn't try to hide it – he doesn't talk about the band or the label, he doesn't even talk to me like a person, he talks at me, like I am a piece of fruit or a scarf. He objectifies me – I don't know, I think that's the technical term. I should be intensely bothered by this, outraged, indignant. But I'm not. I accept it.

'Wynn,' he says. 'Here . . .'

He takes a heavy gold lighter from his trouser pocket and hands it to me. It's warm in my palm.

'Will you light the candle, please.'

It's not a request, it's not an order – but it's, I don't know, it seems natural: He tells me what to do and I do it. There's a candle in a votive beside me on the table. I pick it up, light it, and put it back down.

'No,' he says. 'Put it there.' He points to my lap.

I guess I look at him funny. He sighs.

'Part your knees,' he directs me, patiently, 'place the candle between them and hold it there.'

I do what he says. He seems pleased. His teeth gleam. The candle is scented – ylang–ylang? Mandarin orange? I can feel the heat of the flame on my lips and cheeks. My thighs twitch, clamped on the flickering bowl of wax.

'I like how the light looks on you,' he comments. 'On your face.' He watches me for a while, then says, 'I want to see it on your skin. Why don't you take off your sweater.' Again, not a request.

Holding the candle between my knees and unbuttoning my cardigan is tricky. But he doesn't seem to mind that I struggle with this. When my sweater's off, he extends his hand and I give it to him. He tosses it aside. Then he sits forward, leaning in towards me, his legs now on either side of mine.

'Come closer to me,' he says then. 'Be careful, watch your hair – I don't want to set you on fire.' That last remark must amuse him; he kind of chuckles.

We are close enough to kiss, yet I don't think he's going to kiss me. I have no idea what he intends to do next. And I don't find out.

'What the – Wynn?'

It's Stella. In an instant, she knows what's going on. And she doesn't like it.

'Muthafucka!' she yells. 'What do you think you're doing, you freakin' perv?!'

She's standing right behind me but I don't turn around. Of all people to find me like this – the person I respect, the person that motivates me, the person I really care about. How could I face her? I can't. Instead, I throw up all over Dylan Stoppard's pants.

The Voice

Singing is so simple. When I sing, all I feel is love, coming and going. I give love with my voice, and I receive love from the people who hear me. But being in a band, having a career, all that pesky stuff that goes along with singing? That can be awfully complicated. There are just bunches of things to contend with, it's kind of like a Whack-a-Mole game – you never know when a problem is going to pop up, or who the problem is going to be with, or how it's ever going to get solved.

The night of our showcase, one problem I thought I'd have on my plate was my mom. That had been working my last nerve for weeks. When I'd told her the name of our band, she wrinkled her nose. And after the big dinner party Mr Wandweilder threw, she didn't have anything nice to say about the other kids or their parents. Now, come the showcase, she would not only see the kind of shameless music we do, she'd see me in those high-heel boots she wouldn't buy me. And as if that wasn't spectacle enough, Wynn had to go flash her top.

Backstage, with all those people around, my mom was smiling and friendly as always. And I'd changed back into my sneakers, praying the boots would be an out-of-sight, out-of-mind thing. But I was in a lather over the talking-to she would surely give me once we were alone. I was afraid she'd make me quit the band. As it turned out, though, all that fretting was for nothing. Mr Wandweilder came in, brimming with the news about Flaxxön, and *poof!* My mom may not have approved of 6X or high heels but she did approve of a record deal.

Unfortunately, I couldn't ride that nice feeling for long. *Stomp, stomp, stomp,* the Flaxxön man came tearing down the stairs, Wynn and Stella hurtling after him, stricken as heathens on judgment day. Wynn started to say something – 'Wait, please –' but he cut her tongue out with his scowl. 'You blew it, little girl,' he said.

Each word was crisp as frost, yet at first the simple sentence made no sense to me. It rang in my head as he stormed out the door. 'You blew it, little girl.' What in tarnation? The five little words echoed, over and over, but instead of growing fainter they got louder. And as the volume reached its zenith, a great big 'ohhhh!' of comprehension came over me. Then a bigger, louder, 'ohhh, nooo!' I felt like a Maytag with a chipmunk run amok inside it, while outside of me, the injustice of it all pricked my flesh with the barbs of a devil's pitchfork. This could not be happening – and yet it was. I felt myself propelled in Wynn's direction, though I didn't know what I'd do or say. I really liked Wynn – I'd believed she was a good person. Yet there I was, an inch from her face, demanding, 'What . . . did . . . you . . . do?'

Wynn didn't answer; she just looked away. So I said it again, stronger, *'What . . . did . . . you . . . DO?!'*

Her features hid behind her fringe as she shook her head. All at once her shyness seemed phoney to me, like it was her escape hatch, her way of ducking out when she'd done wrong. 'I – I'm sorry, Kendall,' she said. 'I'm sorry . . .'

'Sorry?!' Oh, something strange and fierce and foul took hold of me. I'd never felt it before but I knew what it was. Hatred. There was hate hissing inside me, shimmying its rattle, opening its jaws to bare fangs dripping venom. I had to get it out – I just had to! So I let Wynn have it. 'You're *sorry?*' I spat. 'You ruined our record deal and all you can say is you're *sorry?* Oh no, *I'm* sorry, but you're not getting away with that.'

The more the hate flowed out of me, the more there seemed to be. It made me shake down to my toes. It blotted out everything else in the room – there was only Wynn, and how much I despised her. 'You think because you have money, because you have that . . . that *body* . . . you have the right to destroy other people's dreams. Good people, hardworking people, people with God-given talent! You think you can just mess everything up and shrug your stupid shoulders and it's OK? No! No, no, no, no, NO! You can't. I won't let you. You're going to own up to this, or . . . or I don't know what I'll do. So you tell me, Wynn Morgan, you tell me right now: What did you DO?!'

The Boss

Maybe one day the image of our angelic frontwoman foaming at the mouth in full-on hissy-fit frenzy will be something I'll look back at and laugh. But let me tell you, at the time it was not cute. At the time, I wanted to kill Kendall Taylor.

'Don't get it twisted, Kendall.' I didn't shout. This stone-cold quiet voice comes out of me when I'm ready to beat a bitch down. 'Wynn didn't do *anything.*'

Kendall wouldn't even acknowledge me; she just kept up her attack. 'I thought you were *nice,*' she raged at Wynn. 'Now I know there's really something *wrong* with you.'

I got right in her face. 'I am warning you, Kendall. You need to shut your mouth before I shut it for you.'

Still, she wouldn't listen. She didn't seem to be aware that she was short-circuiting in front of the adults – and I couldn't believe that none of them, not even Kendall's own mom, made a move to control her. Kendall's cheeks were purple and her eyes bulged as the tirade raged on. 'You act all shy and sweet, but I'm not fooled by that routine anymore. You just want to do as you please and you don't care about anyone else. I can't even imagine what you were doing upstairs with that man, but I do know what you did onstage tonight – everyone's talking about it. You want us to think it was an accident – oh my, my boob popped out! – but knowing the kind of person you really are, I bet you did it on purpose!'

That was the last straw. I raised my arm – to punch her, shove her, decorate the floor with every last one of her pearly whites – but Wynn caught my wrist before I could land a blow.

'But please, no,' she whimpered. 'Stella . . . Kendall . . . please, just stop. You guys don't understand; it's . . .' – she let me go to press her palms against her temples – this girl was coming apart in chunks, headfirst. 'Wait, I want to explain but I don't even understand it myself.'

Tears began rolling down her face, which just made me wanna smack Kendall more. But if Wynn wanted to talk, we had to let her try. I could sense Kendall backing off a bit, and I did the same. Still simmering, we waited on Wynn. Everyone else behind us was holding their breath, taut as stick figures, afraid to blink.

'OK, look, I really am sorry about what I did –'

'You didn't do any –' I started.

'Oh, yes she did –' Kendall sprang.

So much for us backing off.

'No, really – Kendall's right, I screwed up, I screwed everything up for everybody. But it's not that I don't care, I . . .' She trailed off again and moaned. The tears kept spilling; she struggled to speak through them. 'Look, I *know* I'm not worthy of being in a band with you guys. Kendall, you're so gifted, you and A/B, you're artists, real artists. And Stella, you're so determined – you can do anything. Next to you guys, I'm sorry, but I just can't cut it. I mean, I've never actually accomplished anything.'

Wynn's mother tried to interrupt, but my girl stomped her foot to cut her off. 'No, it's the truth,' she went on. 'So I guess on some subconscious level, I screwed things up so the world wouldn't find out what a phony no-talent loser poseur I am.' She wiped her tears with her sleeve and stood up straight. Wynn was owning up, she was being accountable, she was taking responsibility for her actions.

Brava, brava, brava . . .

Trouble was, I didn't believe it, not for one second. That scene with Dylan Stoppard? Wynn just wasn't thinking straight. Maybe she was a little drunk and slipped into a situation – hey, shit happens. No way was she trying to sabotage 6X. Wynn wouldn't do that. She wouldn't, couldn't, do that to *me*.

She pushed her hair out of her face, revealing this steely resignation I didn't recognize. Was it a mask – or how she truly felt? Damned if I knew. Then she picked up her kit bags – cymbals in one, sticks and hardware in the other – and marched over to Kendall. 'You know a lot of talented kids, right, Kendall?' she asked, her voice calm yet weirdly hard. 'Nice kids, worthy kids, kids who eat all their vegetables and do their homework and aren't doomed to burn in hell. Right? Don't you? Well, maybe one of them can play drums.' She dropped the nylon sacks at Kendall's feet with a dull clunk. 'Because I won't be messing up anyone's dreams any more. I'm out.'

PART TWO
Getting Somewhere

'Went down to the crossroads but the devil didn't want my soul/Looks like I'll have to practise if I wanna play Carnegle Hole'

— Tiger Pimp, 'Spurned'

'You're so suicidal/I've felt that way too/I'll be your angel baby/Baby don't be blue'

— N Angel Blue, 'So Suicidal'

'Wonder Bread, Wonder Bread, in the polka-dotted package/Good for breakfast, good for lunch, even good for snackage'

— Windows by Gina, 'Wonder Bread'

PART TWO
Getting Somewhere

The Body

Quitting the band was the right thing. They'd find another drummer. A good drummer. A drummer whose stupid breasts didn't get in the way. They'd probably replace me in a snap – since the showcase came off so well, chicks with sticks would be lining up for my spot. Even if it took a while, there was no rush. Thanks to me, 6X wasn't signing on the dotted line anytime soon.

For me, it would be a relief. No more band business stressing me to the point of insanity. I mean, I just wasn't capable of dealing with it – the pressures, the personalities. And it would only get more intense. We'd done exactly one show, and people were already screaming over us. Eventually 6X would get signed, with me or without me – I was confident of that, this band had something for sure – and with fame and fortune comes incredible responsibility, and always being 'on,' people watching every move you make. Now I could just go back to being the invisible girl.

It was the right thing to do. So how come it felt so wrong? Maybe it was like eating Brussels sprouts or something, I don't know. *Sleep,* I thought, *please just let me sleep, escape.* In the car coming home from Stunt Club, my mom was gearing up a harangue when my stepdad actually shushed her. I remember him going, 'Cynthia, not *now*.' Talk about role reversal. I appreciated that so much. It was as if everything inside me was broken, limping, gasping – somehow my skin held all the pieces in but if I opened my mouth to argue or defend myself or anything, it would be like cracking Pandora's box. All this crazy crippled stuff would come crawling from the wreckage.

I plodded up to my room wearing shoes of lead and flopped on my bed without undressing. Taking a shower would be an Olympian feat. I'd recently regurgitated undigested remnants of Cup 'n' Saucer moussaka and Stunt Club champagne, yet brushing my teeth was out of the question. Sleep, sadly, was equally out of reach. A championship bout between my head and my heart would not be postponed or pre-empted; it was going on now whether I liked it or not. Forcing myself vertical – I didn't want to lie there staring at darkness – I went to light the candles on my bureau and headboard. The second I brought flame to wick, though, I was hurtled back to that fateful balcony scene with the freak of Flaxxön. I *had* to think this through. Forget my horror-movie metaphor about monsters in basements. As the incident unfolded I hadn't thought about the *why*, but there was no escaping it now. Groaning, I groped for my journal. Let me just grab it now; I can read what I wrote.

Possible Reason #1: Boredom.

Bullshit. I was riding a performance high and surrounded by family, friends, bandmates, and a sprinkling of random fabulous people. Ennui had definitely not set in. If I craved amusement, all I had to do was listen to any of Brian's anecdotes. Or ask one of the Tiger Pimps where he bought his scarves. Or change my seat so I could be next to Stella (because being next to Stella, wherever that may be, is always a happy place).

Possible Reason #2: I was drunk.

Except I wasn't. The performance high put my metabolism in overdrive – the two-maybe-more-who's-counting glasses of champagne had zero effect on me.

Possible Reason #3: Dylan Stoppard was a very important man who wanted to sign my band to his label and it was my obligation to be nice to him.

Oh, please! I'd rather call myself a ho than a moron. Being nice means saying please and thank you. It does not mean agreeing to a clandestine rendezvous with some guy, no matter how powerful he is.

Possible Reason #4: Dylan Stoppard was hot and I wanted him.

Hmm. OK. Ouch. Now we're getting somewhere. Somewhere close. Somewhere tender. Dylan Stoppard was traditionally TDH (tall, dark, handsome). Plus, there was something, I don't know, *tasteful* about him. For one thing, he didn't wear any jewellery, not even the requisite earring. Bling on guys is just gross to me. And his manner towards me was understated – interested yet indifferent – and that was intriguing, I guess. He didn't look at me the way other guys did, that whole worshipful, full-yet-hungry thing. He didn't look *at* me at all; he looked *through* me. He didn't see a plastic doll or a goddess or any kind of bad website porn archetype. He saw a sad, clumsy little clown.

He saw me as I saw myself.

That was a first.

So I *wanted* to want him. I wanted Dylan Stoppard to make me feel what no other guy (including my two minimal make-out sessions with different boys) ever had. Guys are supposed to make you feel a certain way, and I wanted . . . *that*. In a club, at three-something in the morning, by candlelight, with everyone I cared about partying obliviously one flight below me, it seemed like Dylan Stoppard could provide. He was different. He had long-fingered hands that held his glass of cognac delicately yet firmly, without any awkwardness. He was a man who knew how to hold things. He was older. Sitting in front of him, doing what he told me to do, I suddenly flashed on Stella, and the way she got when Brian was around. You didn't have to be an empath to pick up that Brian made Stella feel . . . like *that*. Stella glowed in his presence, her body temperature shot up ten degrees when he was in the room. Stella's beautiful, but when Brian's around she's more beautiful. I wanted that. And I wanted Stella to see me have that.

Oh yes. I wanted to want Dylan Stoppard. But when I mused on what it would be like nestled in the crook of his arm, finally identifying what that smell was, the smell that wasn't the cigar in his pocket, that *other* smell . . . that's when I started to gag.

Then Stella walked in, and, well, holy volcano of vomit, Batman!

Fie! Fie! Fie! Which is Shakespearean, I believe, for F – k! F – k! F – k! I'd quit my band, but more than that, I'd quit on Stella, disappointed her, let her down. Most of all, I'd proved her right about me: I was the spoiled lazy rich chick she'd thought I was all along. Quitting was rash, crazy, did-I-leave-my-brain-in-my-other-purse stupid if it meant Stella thinking bad of me.

And with spring break kicking off on Monday, it wasn't like I'd see her in homeroom and we'd talk it out. Did she hate me? Would she ever call me? Should I call her? What could I possibly say? And what about Kendall – there were pretty strong indications that she hated my guts. Did A/B feel the same way, since I'd sunk his rock-stardom battleship with my utter incompetence? What would go down Tuesday afternoon – would those guys get together as usual for practice? Or did my departure mean 6X was broken up?

It was officially tomorrow. Actually, it had been for a while. I dragged myself down to the kitchen and peered out the window. Somehow, life went on. Day maids in uniforms were arriving for work. A squirrel shivered from his perch on a gate across the street. My mouth felt disgusting, and my belly rumbled, but no amount of Ben & Jerry's could answer my questions. So I picked up my journal instead. By Sunday I still didn't have any answers – but I did have a song. I titled it *Bliss de la Mess*.

The Voice

The only thing my mom had to say as we settled into our car service for the ride home from Stunt was, 'Well, thank heaven that's over.' I didn't ask what she meant – but I wondered. Was she glad the long night of fussing and fighting was finally done? Or did she mean 6X was over? I sure hoped it wasn't that. Because even after everything, I did not want to quit the band.

Although it seemed like Wynn had done just that. The way she dumped her drum bags on me as if *her* ruining our record deal had been *my* fault, that was just plain rude. Of course I had blown up at her, but she was being so selfish and unfair. At least I thought she was, I thought she deserved my wrath. That nasty, horrible hatefulness was scary to me, like a sci-fi alien or something. I'd never felt anything like that in all my born days! But once I'd told Wynn off, I got it out of my system. After she slumped out of the club, I started feeling bad – I hadn't been trying to make her leave the band. Really.

The second she left, Mr Wandweilder rushed over and told me not to fret, and Mr Gaylord picked up the drum bags so I wouldn't trip on them. I felt a little better, figuring they'd straighten everything out. Honestly, I didn't want to be bothered by any of it any more. I said good night to everyone as perkily as I could, then conked out in the car before we even got to the Lincoln Tunnel.

The next day, my mom let me sleep past noon, and then I had plans to see the Taras. They're my friends from PEP! – Tara G and Tara S – and I hadn't seen them since I left the squad. We went to the Cineplex for this movie with the Olsen twins, and then got Chinese food. It was nice to have a day off. The Taras didn't even ask me a ton about the showcase. I think they may be a little jealous of me being in a band and performing in New York and all that exciting stuff that they'll never have, but I was happy not to talk about it. Mostly, Tara G wanted to hear about A/B. Tara G had gotten awfully boy crazy lately; she wanted to tell me all about her crushes too – she was in love with two different boys at once.

Then Sunday was pretty typical, church and stuff. My mom and I gabbed about our vacation. She was only working half the week, and on Thursday morning we were set to go down to Frog Level for a visit. She didn't say boo about the band and neither did I, although when a Jessica Simpson ballad came on the radio, she remarked how I could sing rings around 'that reality-show girl.' Was my mom hint-hinting that I go back to that kind of sound? Ooh, it made me cringe inside.

Come Monday, the first day of spring break, I was on my own with nothing to do. I spent most of the day watching TV with the telephone on my lap, hoping A/B would call. We talk on the phone sometimes; he's pretty chatty for a boy. My Friday night fury was not very ladylike – but it *was* kind of rock and roll – and I wondered what A/B thought about all that.

Plus, if he called I knew he'd help me get over the lingering naggy tickles I had about Wynn. There I'd been, thinking Wynn was one way – waltzing through the world without a care – when in fact she was a big old scrambled egg of insecurity. And here I was, without any of her gorgeous, tall, skinny, wealthy advantages – but confidence aplenty. That's all thanks to God, of course. God gave me my talent, and my confidence; He even introduced me to the voice within the voice. I am so lucky. Praise Jesus! Maybe I could talk to Wynn about Jesus and she'd get saved. That would be wonderful!

But how could I? Wynn had quit the band; I would never see her again. I thought about calling her up and pretending nothing had happened – just be my cheerful self – but I got drawn into a soap opera, and then a game show, and then I made a couple of grilled cheese sandwiches and never got around to it.

The phone rang just as I was putting my dishes in the sink.

'Hello, is this Kendall? Kendall, it's Susan in Brian Wandweilder's office.'

I was disappointed. 'Oh,' I sighed. 'Hello, Miss Susan.'

'Hi there, sweetie. Listen, Brian wants me to send a car for you; it'll be there in twenty minutes.'

'A car?' I asked her. 'Why?'

'Brian needs you to come into the city.'

'But . . . why?'

'I don't know, sweetie. But it's very important. Can you be ready in twenty?'

Very important . . . twenty minutes . . .

'Kendall?'

'Oh, yes. Sorry. I'll be ready. Thank you so much for calling.'

She hung up, and I stared at the phone. I had to call my mom . . .

Or did I? True, as my momager, she wouldn't want me making any career moves without involving her. On the other hand she was so busy trying to clear her desk before our trip. So did I really have to disturb her? No, that would be inconsiderate. I changed my shirt, brushed my teeth, and dashed off a note right as the car service pulled up to our house. But once I was halfway inside, I told the driver to wait. I raced back up to my room and fished under the bed for my boots. A very important meeting with Mr Wandweilder? I figured I just might need them.

The Boy

One band's misfortune is another band's lucky break. And if I had to profit off another act's problem I couldn't pick a better one than Angel Blue. Talk about hacks. Angel Blue, the singer chick, used to be in this teenybopper pop trio and all of a sudden she turns punk. Of course, you could sling similar arrows at our frontwoman, but Angel Blue's just a joke. Come on, those interviews she did trying to claim punk cred and then saying she's never heard of the Ramones. Plus, her band's a bunch of pretty boys with matching haircuts and designer tattoos. All forgivable if they didn't have that corp-punk sound that's fingernails on a chalkboard to me. Their last hit single, *So Suicidal*? Let's just say it made me want to jump off a bridge. Last but not least – and I know Stella would slap me for maligning the population of an entire landmass – but they're Canadian.

So when we convened at Brian's office for an emergency band meeting the Monday after our post-showcase debacle and found out we had a shot at replacing Angel Blue on the *Steal This Pony* soundtrack, I couldn't hide my smirk. Apparently poor Ms Blue had a skateboarding accident over the weekend, dislocating a shoulder, cracking a couple of ribs. She'd be in the hospital for a while, and the video for the movie was due to shoot next week, with no wiggle room in the schedule. A substitute was direly needed, and it had to be a teen act since the film was a PG-13 blockbuster boasting half of young Hollywood. Universe, Angel Blue's label, had the soundtrack — and no other rocker kids on their roster.

Here's how fate saved 6X: The music supervisor for *Steal This Pony* happened to be at Stunt Friday night, and she was smitten with us. Especially *Dirty Boots*. As everyone knows now, *Steal*'s about this spunky cowgirl in the big bad gritty city, with a whole kitschy east-meets-western theme. Angel Blue had planned on doing an original of theirs called *Take the Reigns*, but our stripped-down version of the Sonic Youth classic could definitely pinch-hit. You know: boots, dirt — come on, suspend your disbelief.

Still, this music supervisor lacked the clout to convince Keith Leider, the head honcho at Universe, to give us the gig by her say-so alone. So, more serendipity, please: She's at the bar, sucking down Cosmos and complaining about her cloutlessness to none other than my man Gaylord — who just happened to have captured 6X's debut performance for posterity with his camcorder. Armed with that clip Monday morning, it was a hop, skip, and jump to Keith Leider's screening room. Leider was impressed enough to give us a chance — if, of course, we passed an audition.

But before Wandweilder could explain this, some ruffled female feathers had to be smoothed. It was one weird scene — I felt like I'd wandered onto the set of an oestrogen-fuelled reality show. Wynn's already perched primly on the sofa when I walk in. Man, is it tough not to imagine my drummer's bared breast (which to this day I haven't seen, Gaylord's video now locked in Wandweilder's safe at Wynn's behest). Next, Stella saunters in, high-fives me, then transforms into Captain Bligh from *Mutiny on the Bounty,* staring Wynn down like she's the traitorous Fletcher Christian. Wynn gives Stella pleading, stray-kitten eyes, then quickly drops them to examine the pattern on Wandweilder's rug. Last comes Kendall, babbling ebulliently about traffic on the parkway, acting as if she hadn't gone molten on her rhythm section a few days prior.

Brian and I hang back in wary male poses, hoping the girls will sort it out somehow. All he'd done was lay in some convenience-store catering – Red Bull and Choward's Violet gum (Stella staples), Dr Pepper and Butterfinger (Kendall's quaff and candy of choice), and the makings of Pom Spritzers (pomegranate juice and Perrier) for Wynn. Oh yeah, and acid-green Gatorade for me. With Stella planting herself haughtily on top of Brian's desk, and Kendall choosing a chair on the other side of the office, you could cut the tension with a cheese knife and serve it up on Triscuits.

Brian exits briefly and returns hauling Wynn's kit bags. 'I thought you might want these back,' he says.

'Thank you,' Wynn whispers to the rug, daintily taking a strap in each hand.

Endless uncomfortable seconds tick by – and nobody asks why we are gathered here today. So Brian, leaning against the side of his desk not occupied by Stella, elects to spin one of his trademark spiels. 'You know, I don't think I've had the opportunity to tell you guys how awesome you were Friday night. I've seen a lot of bands, and what I saw at Stunt was magic.'

Stella glitters under this praise; Kendall beams matter-of-factly, as if this is nice to hear but also a given. Only Wynn looks completely square-peggy.

'And while whatever happens from this moment on is your decision, and I will respect it, if I could offer the benefit of my experience?' He takes no dissent for assent and continues. 'It boils down to one thing, two words: Bands *fight*. All the time. Yes, the public sees your incredible chemistry and thinks, 'Wow, it's got to be all love with these guys.' But that's just not how it is. The rivalry between Lennon and McCartney? Legendary! The Ramones? Twenty-odd years of chronic loathing. Limp Bizkit, The Vines, The Snooks? All kinds of problems.'

Slowly, the girls start stealing glances at each other.

'What kept them together? You know the answer: The music!' he booms. 'The music, the music, the music!' He pauses to down some bottled water and gauge the reaction to his rock-and-roll bible-thumping. 'So basically all I'm saying is, devastating as what happened Friday night seemed at the time and may still seem now, it could be considered, in the grand scheme of things, not completely insurmountable. I mean, if you want to surmount it, you are mature enough to do so.'

Stella goes first – no surprise there. 'Whatever, people fight, no biggie,' she says. 'I would not be opposed to moving past it, being professional.'

'Well, *I* certainly am a professional,' Kendall says, her eyes on Wynn, not Stella. 'I am also a good person. I believe in forgiveness. The ability to forgive is a wonderful Christian quality.'

Wynn sighs. 'I don't know – I just don't feel like I *belong* here.'

Heatedly, Stella slides off the desk and marches over to Wynn. 'Look, I really don't want to hear any of that "I'm a sucky loser" crap,' she says, then sits on the couch beside her. 'So you're not the best drummer in the world.' Her tone is softer now. 'You get better every day.' She flips back to sass. 'And none of us wants to be breaking in a new girl.'

This makes Wynn crack a smile. 'And if I do start whining, you'll let me know?'

'Oh, you can bet on that,' Stella promises. 'I will figuratively but firmly bust a cap in your ass at the first little sniffle...'

Where's the swell of violin strings? Where are the warm embraces? That's what chicks do, right, kiss and make up? But they don't. They just sit there, exchanging meaningful looks.

'Thank you, Stella,' Wynn says quietly. Timidly, she reaches her hand out and puts it on top of Stella's. 'I . . . you . . . thank you.'

'It's cool,' Stella answers.

'Oh, you guys!' Kendall cries, leaping from her chair and managing to somehow plop herself down between Stella and Wynn, forcing their hands apart. 'I'm so glad you're back, Wynn; I just couldn't imagine 6X without you!' she says. 'Not that I tried, not for one little second!'

Brian claps his hands to interrupt and tell us of our amazing opportunity with Universe. Before he can finish, the girls are gabbing a mile a minute – complimenting each other's outfits like they haven't seen each other in twenty years and gossiping about Angel Blue. Our mission, if we chose to accept it, was to head over to Universe and do an acoustic version of *Dirty Boots* for Keith Leider – at 6:30 that very evening. We had about an hour to pick up our instruments from the practice space (Wynn on tambourine would have to suffice; we weren't about to hump her kit up there) and set it off for the man.

Did we manage it? Well, I'm sitting here talking to a camera in a conference room just down the hall from Leider's corner office, so I think you can answer that one for yourself.

The Voice

The higher the monkey climbs the pole, the more you see his butt. Isn't that a great saying? It's about success – why it's so important to act right the further you go in your career. Not that it's easy! Gosh, after our Universe audition landed us the *Steal This Pony* soundtrack, I was about ready to burst – but when we went down to Frog Level, I didn't show off at all. I was plain old LuAnn again, sitting on my grandparents' porch.

What made it hard was my cousin Carlene. She's only a year and a half older than me but she recently got herself a fiancé. He's this gawky boy who goes to the technical college in Columbia, the state capital – I met him and he was nice enough. She's not actually officially engaged – that boy just gave her a promise ring – yet the whole time of my visit, Carlene behaved all superior to me. Especially when she found out I didn't have a boyfriend and never did have one. You know what I wanted to tell her? That I didn't have time for some foolish boyfriend as I was too busy making a video for MTV. But I didn't. I was humble.

And you know what? I was rewarded. That Saturday morning a FedEx truck pulled up to my grandparents' house;

they never had a special delivery before, so that was exciting all by itself. The deliveryman had an envelope addressed to my mom, and we all gathered around. My grandmomma pulled a hankie from her sleeve to mop her forehead – she was fearing bad news. Instead, it was four tickets to see Alan Jackson and Martina McBride, who were playing that night up in Charlotte – that's in North Carolina, but less than two hours' drive from Frog Level. Orchestra seats, backstage passes, and everything. Mr Wandweilder sent them, with a little letter to my mom urging us to use them if we had a mind to.

Well, Carlene about died. 'Who sent them?' she demanded. 'Who's Brian?'

'Oh, he's just some entertainment lawyer in New York who wants to represent LuAnn,' my mom said, trying to toss it off as no big deal.

'Don't you mean a manager?' Carlene asked – as if she knew something about anything.

'Oh, no,' said my mom, absently fanning herself with the tickets. 'It's a lawyer who's courting her.' .

Carlene gave a hoot. 'A lawyer? Why in the world would LuAnn need a lawyer? What's she done wrong?' That girl wears her ignorance like nail polish.

'Gosh, Carlene,' I said, 'in the music business, if you're trying to get a record deal, a lawyer is the most important thing.' Then I added, 'Of course, there's no way you would possibly know that, so don't feel bad.'

Well, we went to the concert – my mom and I, and my grandfolks. It sure was fun, although that Nashville sound started to work my last nerve after a while. The bands were tight and the performances were bright and shiny, which was kind of the trouble. Where was the edgy, anything-can-happen feeling? I was missing that – bona fide rock chick that I am now. Still, I couldn't wait to go backstage. So after Martina McBride's set, my mom and I left my grandparents in their seats (country people can be shy that way) to see what it was all about.

We didn't see Alan Jackson or Martina McBride – they must have been in their dressing rooms – and it was hard to say if the other people milling around were celebrities or not. One lady looked like a member of SheDaisy, but I couldn't be sure. Most everyone was dressed fancy-casual – ironed blue jeans and sparkly jewelry – and they talked and laughed real loud. It was glamorous, and you needed your laminated badge to be there, yet people seemed to play that down, like, *Oh, we go backstage at concerts as often as we go to the grocery store.* Platters of fruit and cheese were piled high, and men in bolo ties poured drinks – all for free as far as I could tell. I thought about the people lining up to buy corn dogs and sodas at the concession stands. That made me feel special. I reached for a grape.

My mom and I didn't start up conversations with anyone; it was more like an educational experience for us: So this is how the backstage scene is done. Soon enough the lights started flickering on and off to signal that the headliner was about to hit the stage. People began streaming from the area. As we made our way out I spied a large glass bowl full of Hershey's kisses. I dipped in my hand and grabbed a bunch.

My mind began to wander during Alan Jackson's white-hat feel-good honky-tonk. I thought how considerate it was for Mr Wandweiler to send us these tickets. But what my mom said about him courting me? I think he was more courting my mom. After all, before we left for Frog Level she had not agreed to let me go back to the band or be in the video or anything. All she said to him – and to me – was 'we'll see.'

The Body

The Body

The *Dirty Boots* video shoot took place in the fourth, maybe the fifth, ring of hell – actually a cavernous converted warehouse somewhere in Astoria. And an ensemble cast of evil-doers were on hand to help make it happen.

'What am I supposed to do with *this?*' The hairstylist held a lock of Kendall's hair as if it were dusted in anthrax. 'I mean, really . . .' he moaned.

'Don't ask me,' retorted the makeup artist. 'This child must eat chocolate by the crate – her complexion could solve the oil crisis.'

The hair guy was bald as a bead, which seemed suspicious, while the makeup artist, all long neck and tight bun – very wannabe ballerina – had a jumpy, snarky vibe like she ate spiders instead of cereal that morning. Below them, in two director's chairs, sat Kendall and I. I tried to catch Kendall's eye in the long mirrors in front of us, but her head was down. All I saw reflected back at me was the blush of embarrassment rising from her scalp.

'She's greasy at the roots, but the ends are positively parched – I don't think she's had a trim since Britney Spears's first wedding,' the hair guy said. 'And excuse me, I don't cut on set, I'm here to *style.*' He took an exasperated sip of coffee and sighed, but I guess I ought to give him credit: He went at Kendall's coif like he was trying to raise Kurt Cobain's ghost. He tried everything – teased it up, slicked it back, battled her cowlick, and cajoled her split ends. The whole time, an assistant director hovered around, tapping her wrist, which only made the hair guy huffier, 'Will you please stop tapping your wrist at me?' he said testily. 'I know perfectly well what time it is – it's time for me to walk right off this set.'

Neither the hair guy nor the makeup artist did much to me before shooing me off to the costume racks, where I found Stella lying on a bench, straddled by a stylist who yanked at the zipper of Stella's jeans with a pair of pliers.

'Come on, hon, just one more big inhale . . .' the stylist coaxed.

Stella's push-up-bra boobs heaved as she sucked in air. 'That's it! Now hold it!' Somehow the stylist – herself comfortably attired in baggy Dickies and layered tanks – succeeded in zipping Stella into un-prewashed, intentionally too-tight, Western-cut denims. 'There we go!' she exclaimed. 'OK, you can get up now, hon.'

'How do you expect me to do that?' Stella grunted from the bench. 'I can't move. I can't even breathe!'

I guess a giggle escaped me, because both Stella and the stylist looked my way.

'Shut up and help me!' Stella extended an arm. Stifling a second wave of mirth, I grabbed her hand and pulled her upright.

131

'Goddamn!' Stella stood with difficulty. 'Now I know how sausage feels.' She tried to squat and fell down; I laughed and helped her up again.

'Sorry, hon, nothing says sizzle like camel toe,' the stylist shrugged. 'You'll get used to it – and you can pick out any T-shirt you want.' Crossing her arms, she turned her gaze on me, saying, 'Nice, nice . . . I'm thinking early Emmylou Harris meets Daisy Duke. Classy cowgirl crossed with trailer trash. There's a bunch of cute cutoffs and midriff tops on the last rack. Go on,' she shooed me. 'Go try them on . . .'

The outfit sounded skimpy, slutty – not my usual style at all, but perfect for MTV! I wandered obediently toward the farthest rack, ducked behind it ... and was confronted by the sight of A/B, wearing nothing but socks and boxers. I don't know how long I stared. Of course I'd seen guys in swim trunks at the beach, but somehow seeing A/B in his underwear was different. Especially since he had no idea I was behind him. And I admit it, I checked him out. His legs were long and pale but stronger-looking than I'd expected. A decidedly tight butt. Nonexistent hips, lean planes of back and shoulder. As I wondered how peeping on a nearly naked guy was supposed to affect me, I busted out laughing.

A/B swiveled and yelped. Unlike some gross, pumped-up guy, A/B's pecs and abs were naturally defined – his bod had the kind of effortless appeal of someone who doesn't try too hard. Of course, I fixated on his torso since my instinct was to avoid his, um, package. But his hands flew to that area, and my gaze couldn't help but follow.

'Wynn! Shit!' He used one hand to grab better cover – a

cowboy hat large enough to hide behind completely. This led A/B to regain a modicum of composure and all his reliable wit. 'So Wynn, unless you want to engage in a game of "I'll show you mine if you show me yours," do you think you could let me get dressed, please?'

I was glad he made it a joke. 'Sure,' I said, shielding my eyes with my hand as if he was radioactive. 'But can you make it kind of quick? They want me in costume too, you know.'

When I was fully clothed (thankfully, every one of the midriff tops was too small on me, even by MTV standards, so I got to tuck a Western shirt into the cutoffs, a far less slutty alternative), Kendall finally emerged from hair and makeup.

The stylists were right behind her. 'Dear Lord,' the hair guy said to the ceiling. 'I am done.'

One look at Kendall and I had to bite my lip to keep from giggling. Stella was uncharacteristically silent – she didn't make a single sarcastic remark. A/B just looked startled. Kendall's hair was in three little pigtails, one on either side of her head and another poking out at the crown. By now everybody has seen it, of course . . . It made her round face seem chubbier, and with her heavy eye-make-up, powdered-pale skin, and neon orange lips . . . well, it was striking, a look some hard rock harridan like Courtney Love might pull off. But Kendall? Before any of us could react, she was whisked off to wardrobe, squeezed into a fringed top, denim mini, and these crazy cowboy boots – remember how that designer did Timberlands with stiletto heels? Well, now he's gone Western.

The thing about Kendall is, even if she had a moment to complain, I don't think she would have. Poked, prodded, verbally belittled, she endured the most unfair treatment yet still sang her heart out, take after take. She proved what a pro she was – so impressive. Maybe it was a steadfast 'the show must go on' ethos, or maybe deep down she knew that whatever they made her look like, she was Kendall Taylor and that's all that mattered.

The Boss

You wanna know who's a bitch? I'll tell you who's a bitch. Anderlee Bennett – she is the grand freakin' poobah of Planet Bitch. In the movies she's always the popular girl who's actually really nice. Yeah, well, 6X got up close and personal at the *Dirty Boots* video shoot and that girl is a stuck-up, spoiled-rotten, Hollywood-by-way-of-Connecticut bee-yatch.

We thought making the video would be cool, but the vibe was sour from the second we got to the set. Basically, everyone we came in contact with was either an ass or a chickenhead (so-called grown men included). You could've drowned in the Haterade, all right.

I could understand some of the attitude. After Angel Blue bailed, they had to scramble to reconfigure the concept and sizes and shit to accommodate 6X. But please. Concept? Your cat could have come up with it between naps: The band plays *Dirty Boots* while smoke from a machine and fake tumbleweeds blow, and this horse – that's right, a horse: hooves, mane, and manure – walks aimlessly, stupidly, around.

There's not much direct interaction between us and *Steal This Pony*'s stars, TV-heartthrob-turned-movie-stud Reid-

Vincent Mitchell and the afore-freakin'-mentioned Anderlee Bennett. Mostly, they spliced footage of us playing with scenes from the flick. But, well, as everyone who's seen the video knows, we did have two actual scenes with Tinseltown's teen royalty, Reid-Vincent, who, granted, is hot but dumb as your pinky toe, needed to wrap in a hurry, since he was due on location for another movie shooting in Vancouver. Not that the scenes we had with him and Anderlee were complicated. In one, we're not playing our instruments but pairing off in different combinations – me and Wynn, Kendall and Reid-Vincent, A/B and Anderlee – and jumping off this fake cliff they built in the soundstage. That's supposed to represent our sense of freedom. In the other, Reid-Vincent and Anderlee are riding the horse, weaving in and out between us, and Kendall feeds the horse some sugar.

Don't ask me what that is supposed to represent, but whoever thought it was smart to have a horse navigate a rock band in feedback-drenched frenzy ought to seriously consider a career change. Truth: Our yet-to-be-recorded album version of the song will go with the video, but they wanted us actually playing for 'authenticity.' Well, the horse was not having it, so we had to shoot the scene over and over. In one take, the horse decides to eat A/B's hair. In another he rears up and seven – no shit, seven – production assistants run on-set to soothe a freaking-out Anderlee Bennett. But the worst is when ol' Trigger or whatever his name is takes a huge dump in the middle of everything and we have to break to let a cleaning crew come in.

I was with the horse, thinking, *Damn, I did not sign on for this.*

It was tedious, it was tiring, and people treated us like everything that went wrong was our fault. In retrospect, I realize we were whipping boys because we weren't famous yet. We were not Angel Blue, whose first record went platinum; we were just these nobodies. But you know me, I always think who I am, so I did not get this at the time – I expected to be treated with respect and didn't feel I had to walk on eggshells with anyone.

Oops, my bad.

It was sucky enough that the crew was giving us attitude. The stylists were the appetizer course of bitches. The 'concept' required the singer to wear a short, snug skirt (or is there a hoochie union contract clause to this effect?). Well, Angel Blue is a twig and Kendall Taylor is not, which led the stylist to make catty comments under his breath the whole time she was dressing her. And the hair and makeup people kept moaning about us while they were doing us, like we were A) inanimate objects and B) very ugly.

Two hours of hair and makeup later, we were standing around the craft service table, admiring each other while munching carefully to avoid wrecking our primp jobs, when the assistant director pranced over with Reid-Vincent and Anderlee. As he made introductions, Reid-Vincent grunted some monosyllables and fixed his gaze between Wynn's boobs. But Anderlee Bennett made Reid-Vincent's Neanderthal routine seem like a Prince Charming chat-up. She gave us this openly vacant gape – like Con Ed was cranking juice into her baby blues, but no one was home – and then gave us her back.

Her flagrant dis failed to register, though. I wrote it off as a side effect of Xanax or something. I had my rude awakening after the horse dropped his load and a bunch of us wandered back to craft services to sample the new shipment of Krispy Kremes.

'So are movie shoots like this – you do the same thing over and over until a horse takes a crap or something?' I asked Anderlee, who stood nearby, delicately licking the glaze off a donut.

Bitch ignored me. The short hairs came to attention along the nape of my neck. I literally ran my fingers over the spot to calm them, telling myself, *Nah, don't jump to conclusions, Stella. She does not think you are dandruff. She is simply captivated by her Krispy Kreme.*

So I said, 'Because, damn, it is so boring. If that's what acting's like, I'd have to slit my wrists.'

Anderlee turned to me with a cocked head and a sweetly perplexed smile. Then she touched the arm of this woman standing next to her, who must have been her assistant or publicist or some other kind of lackey. 'Jennifer,' she said in that trademark itty-bitty voice, 'will you please tell *her*,' and with the *her* she aimed a finger at me with her free hand, 'not to speak to me. I am having a difficult time as it is and now this . . . person . . . is clouding my aura.'

Jennifer gave me a slit-eyed look.

'It's not fair,' Anderlee continued in cotton-candy tones. 'I told them I had to have my own trailer but they refused, and now look – just *look* – what happens. Anybody off the street thinks they have access. Really, Jennifer, do something . . .'

Jennifer did not have to do something. I did something. I

dropped my donut on Anderlee Bennett's shoes – not as a challenge but out of pure shock – and stepped off, just turned on my heel and walked away. Because if I hadn't, some serious hair-snatching, face-scratching, and bitch-slapping would have gone down, and that would have really thrown off our schedule.

The Body

Outside 6X, everything was rosy. The Universe people were acting as though we'd single-bandedly saved the label. This had Brian and Gaylord bouncing off the walls like jocks on a Budweiser-steroid binge. Internally, though, some kind of mental flu was going around. It was subtle, barely there, like a low-grade fever or an idea you get in the limbo zone right before falling asleep. Maybe it didn't even exist, I don't know. But I sensed it, a simmering strangeness that started at the video shoot and refused to go away.

Take A/B. If he knew you were watching him, he was more rah-rah-arrrrgh than Brian and Gaylord combined. Faking it, obviously – A/B's not a wuss, but he's hardly Mr Testosterone. When he thought no one was paying attention, he shrank inside himself, quiet, even broody.

And Stella? She was this close to a smackdown with Anderlee Bennett, then she just backed off. So not Stella. The horror of the video shoot actually seemed to penetrate her hide, and she didn't snap right back to her old self after. Not that I'd want Stella wounded in any way, but to see her as vulnerable, human . . . it was freaky.

Still, the weird award goes to Kendall. I already said how well she handled herself on set, but soon as we wrapped, she went missing. Which, OK, is not unusual; Kendall's prone to disappearing acts. That day, though, it tried our collective patience – all we wanted to do was say good-bye to those terrible people and get out of there. So we split up, exhausted and annoyed, to search for our errant singer. I stuck my head in the bathroom – 'Kendall? Kendall?' – but she didn't answer. About fifteen minutes later I went in again, because I really had to go.

Checking for a vacant place to pee, I saw the pointy tips of cowboy boots lift hurriedly off the floor. Kendall! She'd been hiding in there all along. I went into the next stall, and tried to figure out what her deal was as I did my business. Well, I could tinkle the Amazon before that would happen. Kendall is . . . un-figure-outable. I wasn't about to pretend that I hadn't seen her, but I was too creeped out to confront her. So I just started babbling aloud, 'Oh, God, Kendall. I am so dying to get out of here – aren't you?'

When I came out, she was by the sink. Hot water streamed from the faucet but she wasn't washing her hands; she was peering at me in the mirror. Her smile was stitched on, her eyes blank as buttons – Raggedy Ann's twin sister, I swear. I didn't even mention how we were hunting high and low for her. 'Come on,' I said, sticking my hands under the tap. 'We've got to give them their stupid costumes back.'

'That's right,' Kendall said. 'We do.'

Flanks of wardrobe racks formed a makeshift changing area. A/B wasn't around; he'd gotten into his own clothes quickly.

Stella sat on a bench, moodily knotting her Doc Martens; she muttered, 'Finally . . .' at our approach. Ignoring her, Kendall and I ducked behind the racks. Kendall turned away from me – she's modest, I guess – and she was dawdling, so I made it fast and gave her privacy.

A styling assistant waited for me, pinch-faced, her hands out. I thrust a bundle at her and she shot me a look.

'Is this everything?'

Did she really think I would steal her precious cutoffs?

'Tori! To-ree!' her boss called pissily. 'Stop gabbing and get this trunk packed.'

The assistant snatched the costume. 'I was not gabbing,' she sniffed, scurrying away.

Soon as the wardrobe witch was out of sight, Kendall emerged from the racks. She dumped a pile of denim and suede on the bench, then headed for the exit and a line of Town Cars ready to drive us home. As I watched her wobble toward a ride, I marvelled at how she still hadn't gotten the hang of high heels. Then it struck me. I couldn't believe it. Kendall was making a knock-kneed run for the border with at least a thousand dollars' worth of designer lizard skin, the sneakers she'd come in with abandoned on the bench.

The Boss

an you believe we had the 'Dirty Boots' video in the can before we even recorded the song? Talk about ass backwards. Universe had this tech whiz who'd sync up our real music to the visuals later. All that seemed to matter was that the clip looked hot – and it did. Even Kendall in her hick-ho outfit and that wacky-tacky makeup job. Lighting and camera angles helped, but I'll admit it: That girl has presence.

So everyone was all happy and shit . . . except me. Shooting that video was like swimming in the infamously filthy waters of Brooklyn's Gowanus Canal – it left this stubborn slime I couldn't shower off. And then having to wait to record? See, Brian wanted a certain room in a particular studio, and it was already booked. Let me tell you, I was depressed. No, I mean it: I would lie in bed all crabby and shit. When Brian suggested a shopping spree to celebrate our video victory, I was just like, whoop-dee-do.

It was the last Friday of spring break. Brian squeezed us in between meetings, but he was so busy we couldn't even go down to the Village or anyplace cool. We met up near his Fifth Avenue office, aka Snooty Store Central. Silky as a shampoo ad, security not even blinking as she glided by, Wynn wandered the counters at Saks Fifth Avenue, idly fondling the merchandise, buying nothing. Kendall discovered Coach and tricked herself out with a purse, wallet, and key chain. A/B got geeked in The Sharper Image.

Brian watched 6X spend his paper like he was Willy Wonka, and Rockefeller Center was his chocolate factory. Too corny. I couldn't take it – I went outside and sat on a wooden bench, trying to stare down the atmosphere. Technically, it was a beautiful day. Warm enough to wear just a hoodie. Bright sunny sky. Daffodils and tulips lined up in planters like the freakin' Rockettes. But all I could see were irritating tourists mingling with equally irritating suits, posing for snapshots, yammering into cell phones, and basically getting in my face.

Uch.

I caught a glimpse of Kendall in Coach's window as she deliberated baby blue versus powder pink. A satisfying fantasy came to me: I storm into the store with a paintball arsenal and splatter the preppy pastel accessories and salespeople and not-so-innocent bystanders with a thick assault of vomit green. The daydream faded rapidly, though. I just couldn't hold on to anything good.

That's when Brian materialized next to me. I kept my focus straight ahead. I was more pissed at him than anything else – don't ask me why. The suckage of the video shoot wasn't his fault. Maybe I'd just reached my limit in terms of band togetherness. Couldn't Brian find thirty freakin' minutes to see me solo? We could do it on the low – I know he can't play favourites, let those guys see him treating me special. But half an hour after work, him and me, trawling the Bleeker Street flea market. Quality time.

'What's the matter, Stella — the firm's money not good enough for you?' he wanted to know.

I didn't even sling him any snark. Truly, I couldn't give two shits.

'Look, I know I said this was a celebration, but the fact is I'm trying to make it up to you guys — I heard the video shoot was not exactly a day at the beach.'

I just snorted, then burned this thought into him: *Forget about it — this is me, Stella Anjenue Simone Saunders, and you can't buy your way into my good graces.* I could practically feel his heart and brain conspiring on what to say to make things right. *Fine,* I thought. *Suffer.* Just then, this bimbo with a bottle tan and a drop-kick dog in her purse walked by. I shook my head and muttered. Brian had the exact same reaction. Behind my shades, I sneaked a look at him.

'See, that's what I mean — that's what surprises me,' he said.

What the hell was he talking about?

'Nothing escapes you, Stella, right? So frankly I'm stunned that out of all you guys, you're the one not taking this in stride. Are you really upset that you weren't treated like royalty at your first video shoot?' He snapped his fingers, the way I do — only his snap isn't as sharp. 'Wake up and smell the horse shit, Stella.'

I almost cracked a smile, but I wasn't quite feeling it. Only a smirk appeared.

Brian took that as his licence to continue. 'There's only one reason to do what you're doing: You love playing music in this band. It's all about the process – onstage, at practice, in the studio. The rest of it is crap. You have to keep it in perspective.'

Arms crossed, legs apart – his pose was just like mine. He let his lecture fly.

'Those people at the shoot?' he said. 'Tip of the iceberg. Wait'll you're officially signed. Your A&R person, your advocate at the label who's supposed to look out for you, nurture your talent, protect you from the fascists? Well, A&R is supposed to stand for "artists and repertoire" but you'll soon find out it means assholes and retards. And don't get me started on the sycophants.'

I looked at him full-on for the first time that day. He didn't miss a beat. 'Publicists, product managers, journalists,' he explained without explaining. 'Today's butt-kissers, tomorrow's backstabbers.'

Suddenly he stopped talking. He must have realized that he couldn't tell me a thing – I'd have to figure it out my damn self. He lowered his gaze from the sky-scrapers to the street, and we both sat quietly. After a while he nudged me in the ribs and leaned close to my ear. I couldn't help it – I felt my shell crack. 'Check it out,' Brian whispered. Standing to our left was this . . . vision. Ballet flats, balloon pants, poufy-sleeved shirt, hoop earrings. The lady looked like an extra from *Pirates of the Caribbean*. 'All she needs is the eye patch.'

'And the wooden leg . . .' I added.

We snickered privately. We sat a little closer. Around us, the crowd surged and swirled, yet it felt like we were alone, or invisible, or a different species. The foggy funk I'd been breathing in for days miraculously lifted all at once. I sucked in some fresh midtown Manhattan air and let my head fall on Brian's shoulder. It fit there perfectly. It really was a beautiful day.

The Boy

There's nothing fake or slick about Brian Wandweilder. And he's not a forceful, intimidating guy either. He doesn't wrap you around his little finger or pummel you into submission with his fist. But man, he could sell Goldschlager to Straightedgers, suntans to goth kids, polo shirts to punks. It could be his earnest enthusiasm – he wants something so bad and believes in it so completely, he convinces you to go along. Or maybe he's just a natural born sizer-upper: He figures out in a heartbeat what you crave or fear most and speaks straight to that. If you're insecure, he feeds your ego; if you're a tough guy, he shoots from the hip; if you fancy yourself a comedian, he laughs at your jokes – by giving you what you need, he talks you into anything.

Still, I think the hardest nut he ever had to crack was JoBeth Taylor, Kendall's mom. She's another one I can't figure out – the strangest stage mother on earth. She wants Kendall to succeed, but at the same time she resists Wandweilder's every manoeuver. It's insane. Kendall told me that she doesn't get it either.

One day, though, Brian took the lady to lunch. The next day he was like Achilles at Troy. The conquering hero. Not only did he nudge Mrs Taylor into OK-ying the Universe deal, he pulled off another enormous coup regarding her daughter's day-to-day routine. Next semester, Kendall will switch from regular high school to a private tutor, at the label's expense. And Universe will spring for something else too. It's a good label, an understanding label; it knows how difficult it is to commute into the city for all the things a soon-to-be-rock-star must do. Hence, Kendall will be moving into an apartment of her very own, fourteen doorman-building floors above Manhattan's creatively inspiring and ever-happening East Village. Niiiiice . . .

The Voice

So many incredible things I never even dreamed of started happening all at once. The video, of course. A movie premiere – 6X was invited to the *Steal This Pony* party. My own apartment – oh sweet Jesus. My mom was OK about the place because it's in the Teen Towers. Oh, it's not really called that on the entrance or anything, but a number of young actors and musicians do live there. The building even has on-staff chaperones for when parents themselves can't be on the premises. It's pretty fancy – the lobby has purple carpet and smoky glass – but my mom tried her best to get me the nicest apartment there.

Sweet as pie and strong as steel, that's my mom. 'Oh, this is a cute little place – but I doubt it will do for Kendall,' she told the estate agent when we came to give it a look-see. 'My daughter, Kendall Taylor? She simply has to have southern exposure. She's a singer, you know – lead vocalist for 6X? – and singers need plenty of sunshine. I'm sure Keith Leider, the president of Universe Music? Well, he wouldn't want his brightest new star in a *gloomy* apartment.' She was knocking on walls, taking measurements with her mind, and saying stuff like,

'This is the only closet? Oh, it's perfectly nice and all, and I'm sure it's big enough for the average teenager. But I can't tell you how many clothing companies have been in touch about endorsement deals! Plus, you know how designers are about showering celebrities with gifts they can be seen in? It would only be a matter of time before Kendall was bursting out of this tiny thing. There just must be an apartment with a walk-in.'

It was cool listening to my mom negotiate. All that talk of endorsement deals, well, it was the first I'd heard of it. Certainly no designer had given me so much as a sock (unless you count those boots from the video shoot – surely Manola Blahnik *wanted* me to have them, since he didn't ask for them back). Not that my mom was lying; as she said it was only a matter of time – and it made me sound important. Gosh, I'm lucky to have such a smart mom. The arrangement we have is that I'll stay at the Teen Towers when I have business in the city, which is most of the time, lately; otherwise I'll be in New Jersey and just be normal. My mom allowing me to do this really shows how much she trusts me and believes in me, and that's such a good feeling.

It shows how much Universe believes in me too, since they agreed to foot the bill before 6X was even signed. Our actual recording contract was contingent on how good *Dirty Boots* came out. At that point, the label had us on a development deal, which basically kept other record companies from poaching us. Honestly, it was all pretty complicated and I was glad I didn't have to concern myself. All I had to do was sing.

But the apartment wasn't even the best part. Someone who doesn't know me might think all I want is fame and fortune, but the truth is I am simply a regular girl. I yearn for the same things all high-school girls yearn for. And yes, I can be a little uncertain about those things. With my singing I am very confident because I trust completely in God and His gift to me. But with some things – personal things, social things – I'm as insecure as the next person.

Things like knowing whether or not a boy likes me. That can be awfully tough to tell, since boys never want to show their feelings. But now I know for sure that A/B does. Like me, I mean. He must. Because the other day after the shopping spree, we were walking downtown together – I was headed to catch my bus at Port Authority, and he was off to Penn Station for the train. Now I have this trick for talking with A/B, so there won't be any awkward silences: I ask him about school stuff – since he's a senior, he's an expert on everything I'm going through as a sophomore. Smart, isn't it? That afternoon, I asked him about geometry.

'Couldn't tell you, Kendall,' A/B replied. With so many people zigzagging on the street, I wished we were holding hands. 'Soon as I walked into trig as a junior, geometry was erased from the blackboard of my brain.'

'Oh, that's all right,' I said, then followed up – that's very important when talking to boys, asking lots of questions. 'It must be wonderful not having to take maths at all this year. Don't you love being a senior? What's the best part?'

'It's all right,' he said, shrugging. 'I'm kind of . . . detached.'

'Gosh, I can't even imagine that,' I told him. 'Personally, I've got tons of school spirit.' We had reached 42nd street – the place where we part ways – but I so wanted to talk to him more. I tugged his sleeve. 'In fact,' I said, 'it makes me sad when I think about next year, me being with a tutor and all that.' It was so busy on the pavement – they don't call Times Square the crossroads of the world for nothing – that I had to shout.

'Oh, come on Kendall, don't be sad,' A/B shouted back. 'It'll be great, I promise. No smelly cafeteria. No getting a pass every time you need to pee. No gym!'

I smiled at him – he really was trying to make me feel better. 'But no football games? No homecoming? Worst of all, no prom?'

He shrugged again. 'Is that really such a big deal?'

Now this shocked me. Even the special-ed kids know that prom is the pinnacle of the high-school experience. 'A/B Farrelberg, don't be ridiculous!' I exclaimed. 'You know perfectly well that prom is simply the best night of your life. For a girl it is, anyway. The dress, and doing your hair up special, the corsage . . . and, well, everything.'

'No shit?' he said, glancing left and right. I tugged his sleeve again so he'd look at me. 'Well, if it's that much of a hoo-ha, you want to go to mine?'

Right then it felt like an earthquake was hitting Times Square. I had to concentrate to keep my feet planted and not go crashing into the window of BubbaGump. Neon pulsed around us – I could almost hear it buzz. 'Your . . . ?'

'The prom thing,' he said. 'You want to go?'

'A/B!' I cried, and grabbed both his arms, because if I was about to go crashing into the window of Bubba Gump, I wanted him with me. 'You have just made me the happiest girl in the whole entire world!'

The Boy

The next time the band got together, it was in a holy place. Hit Factory, the legendary studio with the ever-so-apt name. If those acoustically perfect walls could talk – they wouldn't talk, they'd sing. I wasn't dreaming – I'd pinched myself – I was really there, recording *Dirty Boots*, the single to the *Steal This Pony* soundtrack, brought to you by those fine, fine chart-busters at Universe Music.

Yeah, the scheduling was screwed up, us doing the video, then having to go back to school for a few weeks after spring break, then blowing off school for the recording sessions. It didn't really bother me. Graduating high school was the least of my worries.

Once we were in the studio, all I thought about was *Dirty Boots*. Alan Slushinger and I worked out my guitar solo in painstaking detail; I'd play it, he'd listen, we'd tweak. The sound in that room! It was multiple sonic orgasms for me.

'OK, so forget everything we rehearsed,' Alan told me when it came time to lay down my licks.

I was so astounded I dropped my pick.

'No, seriously,' he said. 'You have the skills, Grasshopper, you're in top form. But it has to be spontaneous. You don't want to lose the rough edges. It is, as the poets say, only rock and roll . . .'

'Yeah, but . . .' But what? 6X couldn't have asked for a better helmsman than Slushie. He'd produced all the Windows by Gina records and a handful of other cool artists as well. The guy has great ears, great instincts – he'd done an awesome job on the song so far. The bass and drum tracks boomed and rumbled like Armageddon coming – you could *smell* them. The feedback infused over my main guitar lines was bitter, buzzy, brilliant. And the vocals? Slushie worked till the wee hours coaxing stuff out of Kendall that just had me awestruck – she sounded innocent and menacing and ferocious and wasted all at the same time. The tune was virtually finished; all we had left was my solo. Slushie was the man – I had to trust him.

'Dude, don't worry,' he assured me. 'We have plenty of time – and plenty of tape. You're going to nail this sucker.'

And I did. About seventeen times. Each time I played the solo it sounded slightly different – and self-aggrandizing asshole I may be, amazing. I didn't know how we'd choose a version to go on the track.

So I was on top of the world. Except I was completely out of my mind. As long as I had my trusty Dan Electro in hand, I was fine. But as soon as I stopped playing, my brain flipped back to berserk. Earlier that year I'd applied to a couple of colleges like the NJB that I am. That week, I'd learned the good news: I'd been accepted to both. And I'd made a decision: I wouldn't be attending either one. I just didn't know how to break this to my parents. It would kill them. Or they would blame – and kill

155

– each other. Or they would join forces and kill me. A bloodbath would ensue, any way I looked at it.

What's more, I wasn't thinking straight about other stuff and managed to fall into a huge vat of shit. I am going to have to do something absolutely anathema to me, something I swore I'd never do. And I am trapped, treed, cornered, caught. My fate is sealed – there is no squirming out of this one: I will be going to *prom*.

The Voice

Recording is real hard work! At the *Dirty Boots* sessions, Mr Slushinger kept wanting to hear different versions – he'd say things like, 'This time, make it greasy,' or, 'Sing it from your secret place.' Of course I gave it one hundred and ten percent, but it was such a chore, and while I wouldn't dream in a million years of being rude to my producer – or to anyone, really – sometimes a little sass sneaked out. And hoo-wee, if the sessions went late and we ran out of Dr Pepper? That happened once and I got so mad; I made the studio intern go out and fetch me some, and when he bought diet instead of regular, well, I hate diet soda, it tastes funny, so I had to make him go out again.

It's the principle of the thing. I'm Kendall Taylor and I should have what I want. I'm becoming a star now, and I expect to be treated like one. I will *not* let people walk all over me. Like at the video shoot, when I took those boots. I was just so peeved by how mean those people treated me – how dare they!? Even though I had to hole up in the bathroom for twenty minutes to muster the nerve, well, those boots are mine now. And every time I wear them, I get this inner 'hmpf,' like I showed them!

Bedsides, it's important for a high-profile person to look paparazzi-ready at all times. Trouble is, I could probably use a little help in that area. Because there have been times when I've read *Teen People* – that 'yeah, yeah, yuck' page, where they rate celebrity fashion – and I actually like the 'yuck' better than the 'yeahs.' It would be so, so, so mortifying to end up there.

So I decided to go to Wynn. She really knows about the finer things. We were sitting in the posh reception lounge at Universe, waiting for them to give us a sneak peek at the video synced up to our single. Gosh, it was pins and needles time – we'd heard MTV was crazy about the clip, and we were all excited about the airdate. But A/B was late, some kind of derailment on his train from Long Island. Fortunately, this very efficient intern in publicity was catering to us, bringing us magazines and taking drink orders, and when I told her I was famished she said she knew where someone kept a stash of M&Ms. Since it was just us girls, I figured I'd take advantage and get some fashion advice. I went and sat near Wynn, and said, real casual, 'Hey, can I ask you a question?'

She licked cappuccino foam from her lip and said I sure could.

'Well,' I said, 'I've been wondering about the *Steal This Pony* premiere, how fancy it's going to be and what I should wear.'

Stella looked up from her magazine, disgusted. *Steal This Pony* was her least favourite subject. 'Who gives a shit? None of those movie people give a good goddamn about us; the premiere is just gonna be paparazzi for *J-14* and shit. Me, I intend to roll up in jeans – and they can kiss my black ass if they don't like it.'

Then, if you can believe it, Stella actually lay down on the sofa like she lived in the Universe lounge, her sneakers on the cushions and everything. She reopened her magazine. End of discussion. As if I was even speaking to her. I looked at Wynn.

'Actually, I think Stella's right – you can pretty much wear what you want,' she said. 'Look at *In Style* – the stars show up to the red carpet in everything. You could put on jeans and a fancy top and be perfectly fine. Or you could wear a nice dress. Or you could go all-out and wear a designer gown.'

A designer gown, I thought. That would be wonderful. 'Have you decided what you're going to wear?'

Wynn sipped her cappuccino thoughtfully, 'Not really,' she replied, 'but now that you mention it, hmmm . . .'

I imagined her flipping through her closet in her head, mentally reviewing scads of skirts and dresses and shoes.

'I'll probably go the nice dress route,' she said upon completing her inventory. 'Not that I have anything I like. Guess it's time to get mom to hand over the Gold Card.' Wynn blew at her fringe. 'She will be so thrilled.'

Well, I doubted my mom had a Gold Card to hand over but I figured she'd let me buy something new for a special event. Knowing my mom, though, she'd insist that whatever I got for the premiere I'd have to wear for A/B's prom too. She's just dyed-in-the-wool thrifty. Which simply compounded my problem – I'd have to find one outfit suitable for both occasions.

'Wynn . . . ?' Oh, I hoped she'd help. 'You think we could go shopping together? I'd really value your opinion, especially since whatever I buy for the premiere I'll also have to wear to A/B's prom and –'

'What?' Wynn flicked her head like there were moths in her ears.

'WHAT?' shrieked Stella from the sofa. So much for her being too cool for our conversation. She got up and marched over, and crossed her arms over her chest.

I looked back and forth between my two bandmates.

'Be real now.' Stella loomed over me. 'A/B? Going to *prom?*'

'Stella . . .' Wynn said, as if trying to avert trouble.

But there was no stopping Stella.

'With *you?*' she said. 'No freakin' way . . .' Then she started cackling.

The Body

Shopping with Kendall was . . . interesting. The things she picked out. Hideous. Bows on top of bows. Spangles with sequins. I tried to guide her but she is terminally tasteless.

'How about this?' I proffered a simple crepe de chine. A-line cut with an empire waist. It would flatter her shape.

Kendall crinkled her nose. 'It's so plain,' she said. 'And so . . . *black*.'

She pulled out a fuchsia-and-turquoise chiffon monstrosity and held it against her. I sighed. It was no use. Then she saw the price tag and gagged. We decided to check out a different department, and while waiting for the lift, something remarkable happened.

This girl came along to the lifts. She must have been about twelve, and built like a barrel, round and ungainly. As her oblivious mother rattled into a cell phone, this tween riveted on us – on Kendall, really. Openly agape, eyes the size of cupcakes, she raised her arm and pointed her finger.

What's this kid's deal? I wondered.

But Kendall knew. She tilted her head and smiled warmly. This made the girl freak even more, and when Kendall walked

161

up to her, I thought we'd have to call 911. A squeak came out of the girl. Her entire body began to tremble. She was having paroxysms, a seizure, I swear. I couldn't hear what they were saying – they were a good fifteen feet away from me – but Kendall and the little barrel girl were both beaming like satellites.

Then the girl began yanking her mother's arm, so hard the woman almost lost her cell. Yet after the tiniest flicker of anger, the mom seemed almost as excited as her daughter. She opened her bag and rummaged blindly inside, never taking her eyes off Kendall. Out came a pen and a bunch of envelopes – bills, invitations, whatever. Kendall accepted one, scribbled on it and handed it to the girl. When she leaned down to place peck on cheek, the kid threw her meaty, freckled arms around Kendall's neck and hung on. The other people at the lifts were watching by then. You could feel the whole area buzzing.

I am so dense. The scene unfolded right in front of me, yet it took me forever to grasp that Kendall had just been recognized by a fan. She'd signed an autograph – the first of many.

Surreal as it felt, it did make sense. The *Dirty Boots* video debuted on MTV that week – promo for *Steal This Pony,* set to open the following Friday. And it was a hit. An instant hit. Sure, it had the Hollywood power push behind it; that's how it got introduced on *Brand Spanking New.* But no one counted on it taking off the way it did.

By now, everyone knows it; it's still on *TRL.* And of course 'The Kendall' – the look she sports in the clip – caught on the second *Dirty Boots* dropped, Three-pronged pigtails, defiant miniskirts, orange lipstick. At long last, size 16 has a role model.

Even if you don't wear the look yourself, if you've ever felt too fat or too dumb or too anything or not anything enough, you look at the mitosis of 'The Kendall' on every street in every town and you think, *Yeah*.

Oh, and all those girls who always felt cool and thin and privileged and pretty, just so above it all – the plastics and the perfects – they look at 'The Kendall' and, whether they admit it or not, they get a little nervous.

The Boy

Ti-yiii-yee-ime was on my side, yes it was.

Right after we mixed *Dirty Boots*, the single magically appeared on the Internet. No, really, I don't know how it got there but I suspect the fiendishly brilliant Gaylord Kramer had something to do with it. Anyway, there it sat for a couple of days collecting cyberdust. Then the video made its *Brand Spanking New* debut and a downloading frenzy began. The response was so enormous, Keith Leider, majordomo at Universe, bumped everything on his schedule to allow him and Brian to work out the details of our deal. Two albums, massive tour support . . . no, no, I cannot divulge how much dinero.

I really hope the amount doesn't leak. People will be grousing about 6X enough – overnight sensation sour grapes. And OK, maybe we did come out of nowhere, maybe we did luck into the right legal representation, maybe Wynn and Stella can barely play their way out of a paper bag. So what? Maybe the cosmos aligned in our favour because we want it, we deserve it, we work our butts off, and we can go note-to-note with any piece of alternacrap the industry spins out. That's how I like to think of it, anyway.

The bonus? It gave me the best excuse ever to tell my parents I'd be blowing off college: A mumble-mumble-mumble dollar recording contract.

The Boss

Sushi, jumbo shrimp, crab claws, lobster tails – there was more damn marine life at the *Steal This Pony* premiere party than at the Coney Island Aquarium. For carnivores, a roast beef big as a brontosaurus was carved to order by this dude in cowboy gear. Cauldrons of chilli and vats of guac pushed the Western theme, as did the hors d' ouevres – mini quesadillas and tiny tacos. Plus pastries and cookies, fist-sized strawberries dipped in chocolate, and buckets of exotic fruit. Quite a spread, let me tell you.

The movie – shocker – sucked royally. But I somehow survived Anderlee Bennett and Reid-Vincent Mitchell's performances, and then we all piled into a limo for the soiree. In spite of myself I had a blast. Our video had blown up by then, so everybody wanted to meet us. Photographers snapped our pictures and journalists with and without minicams asked moronic questions like what did we think of the flick and how did it feel to burst onto the scene.

Reid-Vincent Mitchell had flown back from Vancouver for the event, and he was acting like him and 6X were buds since birth. Even that hater Anderlee Bennett was on her best behaviour, posing with her arms around us. Phony little bitch. The whole affair was revolting, but it was a real crash course in showbiz shenanigans.

I strutted around like I owned the place, Wynn clinging to me like lint. It's funny, she's all rich and hot looking, you'd think she'd be in her element, but she was like the mouse at the cat convention. She grabbed my hand and let me lead the way through the throng. It was crazy ironic – here's this babe every dude in the room is drooling over, and she's glued to me.

Piloting around, I scoped out A/B. I hadn't had the chance to give him shit about his upcoming prom date yet. But when I located him hanging with Brian, all at once I lost the urge to dis him. A high-school dance? It was too immature to bring up in front of Brian.

The four of us stood there, scarfing strawberries and making chitchat, and all at once I was overwhelmed wishing it could just be Brian and me, off alone somewhere, watching the circus, spitting comments, above it all. I was about to propose it too – just get on tiptoe and whisper it in his ear – when that annoying Denni, Danni, the Web gossip queen, swooped down on us in a too-tight T-shirt, tiered mini, polka-dot tights, and a plastic pail intended for sand-castle building as her freakin' bag. 'Oh, my favourite little darlings on earth!' she shrieked. 'How much do I love 6X? How brilliant and genius are you? I must get a picture for the site. Where's my photographer . . . ?'

PART THREE
Real Time

'My body – my decision / I defy your X-ray vision / Don't stalk me with
your hungry stare / That's why it's called underwear'
                                            – '(I Am Not a) Lingerie Model'

'Somewhere west of Amsterdam / How can you know who I
am? / Daddy, I don't give a damn'
                                            – 'My Real Dad Lives in Prague'

'Uch! Scat! Shoo! I don't care how popular you are – I can't stand
you!'
                                            – 'Hello Kitty Creeps Me Out'

Lyrics by Wynn Morgan

Music by Morgan / Saunders / Taylor / Farrelberg (HotShit Music-BMI)

The Boss

Enough backstory already. Enough about how we hooked up and got started and shit. We've inked our deal; we're officially starting to record our debut. We're in real time now — for real. Present freakin' tense.

As usual, though, there are issues. The supply and demand thing — that's major. See, thanks to *Dirty Boots* blowing up, we're in demand but, oops, no supply. It's bananas: We're this famous band but we only have one song out . . . We only *know* four songs total. So the idea is to make us as visible as possible while working to crash our album A-SAP.

Keeping us in the public eye is top priority at Universe. Our A&R guy, Preston Schenk, he is one shrewd mo-fo. He also A&Rs Windows by Gina — yeah, we're labelmates now — and part of his plan for world domination is to have Kendall guest star on their next single, *Wonder Bread*. They'll remix the tune with her additional vocal track, plus she'll be in the video. The strategy is to move in on WBG's audience — they're big with the college-and-up crowd, so we'll be exposed to older people who might actually go out and buy CDs instead of downloading everything like kids do. Truth? It bugs the shit out of me that

Lil Miss Freak Show gets to do this, but I have to push past that. It's for the good of the band.

As for the rest of us, we've got a minitour on tap: Boston, Atlanta, Chicago, LA. Key cities. We'll play, schmooze, visit radio stations. Phoebe Stones, our publicist, she's booking us on TV too. Conan O'Brien looooves us; we're definitely gonna do his show. Plus, Phoebe's wrangling us invites to every high-profile young celeb event in New York – it's all about mingling with the camera-ready crowd.

What else? Oh, yeah, our website. Gaylord found this guy, Nathan DaWeen. Ha, DaWeird is more like it. Lazy eye, bushy beard, sleeps in his clothes. But what's a little body odour? DaWeird promises to get our site up stat. Then we'll be able to connect with the masses. And they'll be able to connect with us.

The Body

Look at my nails. Oh God, don't – they're so disgusting. I can't stop biting them. We did this rush-job photo session – the label's publicity department was desperate for images – and I kept my hands in my pockets the whole time. I am such a wreck these days.

School is strange. Some people are catty and obnoxious, others are fawning all over us, like, 'Wow, you're on MTV.' Not only is it embarrassing, it's distracting. Focus? What's that? Stella doesn't have this problem. Despite all the band stuff, she's flying through Flex-Learn; she already aced her SATs and if she takes some coursework over the summer, she'll be a full-fledged senior in September at the ripe old age of sixteen.

Last Saturday was her birthday, in fact, and we were in LA. We get there Friday and check into the Villa Chin-Chilla, this hipster hotel on Sunset. Kendall is obsessed with the minibar. Every time she takes a piece of candy she announces how much it costs: 'This Toblerone is ten dollars!' The rooftop pool is a total scene, but I'm so fried after one No-Hito I have to crash. I have no idea how late the other guys partied.

Saturday afternoon, we play a mall in the Valley and then do an autograph signing. Tons of kids show up, it's lunacy. All these girls dressed like Kendall – so cute. That night we play the Whisky. A/B is so excited – it's such a hallowed hall – I swear, I think he's going to lick the floor.

The Whisky show is the complete opposite of the mall. Snark-mongers, elbow-rubbers, Hollywood's edgy elite. Journalists come, the label's entire West Coast office, all the right celebs. At the post-gig meet-and-greet, we chat with Crimson Snow and Jake Pfstadd, indie flick icons and celeb couple of the moment, so that's our coolness seal of approval right there.

After that, we celebrate Stella's birthday – the band, Brian, some Universe people, and Stella's mom. (To keep expenses down, the rule is one designated parent per away show; as mom of the b-day girl, Mrs Saunders had dibs on LA.) We go to the Mahogany Room – black-and-white glossies of dead movie stars, a gigantic crystal chandelier, very kitsch. The entertainment is Sheldon and Sheila, this lounge act. He sports a velvet jacket and plays piano; she's in evening gown and tiara, and she sings. They've been married a hundred years. Between numbers, they bicker – it's hilarious.

All of us being underage, Brian or whoever had to pull some strings to even get us in. No one drinks alcohol, but I'm not sure if that's out of deference to us or typical California health consciousness. A cake with sixteen lit sparklers is wheeled out on this cart, and Sheldon and Sheila lead us in *Happy Birthday* and *16 Candles*, only we sing '16 sparklers . . .'

Then it's time for gifts. The Universe people ceremoniously present Stella with an iPod, and the head of West Coast promotion jokes that they programmed it with the label's entire catalogue, surely the only tunes she'll ever need. She gets a tennis bracelet from her mom – it seems more Mrs Saunders's taste than Stella's – and Kendall gives her candles shaped like angels. Candles, fine. But angels? For Stella? A/B's gift is actually adorable – this Taurus T-shirt with a bull prancing in a field of daisies – but also a little on the girly side for Stella.

It just seems to me that if you're going to give someone a present, you should think about what they'll really *like*. I'd sweated over my gift: a silver skull thumb ring with green stones for eyes. Stella does seem to dig it; she leans over the table to kiss me thanks, then sticks it on her finger. Brian's gift is the best, though. You know how Stella worships the Ramones? Well, somehow he found a vintage leather jacket signed across the back by all the band members. She's floored. And then he makes this incredibly sweet toast about the first time he met her and how she continues to rock his world on a daily basis. Such a Kodak moment.

Brian actually blushes, I swear, when he and Stella hug and we all clap. Stella looks so happy – her smile, her eyes, her *earlobes* are aglow. I'm happy, too – happy for her, happy for 6X. Yet this lump of melancholy wells up in my throat, making it impossible for me to speak, and I don't know why. When Sheldon and Sheila propose a round of *You're Sixteen (You're Beautiful and You're Mine)*, I can only mouth the words.

The Boy

They don't call the night flight from LA to NYC the red eye because attendants dole out hydroponic happy sticks with each little package of peanuts. It takes off at ten PM and lands at Kennedy around six in the morning, so the nickname refers to passengers not getting any Zs along the way. In our case, however, sleep seemed like it might be an option: We're not rock starry enough for first class yet, but the plane wasn't full, so each one of us claimed an entire row in economy to stretch out.

But can I catch a nap? No way, man. I find myself spending the flight in a new role – rock-and-roll rabbi.

'Dude . . .' A hoarse whisper wafts toward me. 'Hey, you up?'

'Yeah . . . yeah . . .' My vision adjusts to the darkened cabin. 'Hey, Stella.'

'Come on, sit up.' Rapping my shoulder, she slips in beside me. 'I wanna talk to you.'

'Yeah, sure.' I wonder how bad my breath is and reach into my pocket for gum. I take a piece, offer Stella a stick. An

Anderlee Bennett movie drones on the monitor several seats ahead of us. 'So . . .'

'So? So tell me all about it, Prom King.'

I groan. I knew Stella would give me shit about the rite of passage upon which I am about to embark – I just don't know what took her so long. 'What can I say, Stella?'

'Say it isn't true – you'wouldn't be caught dead going to prom.' She snaps her gum. 'And above all, say you're not taking Missy Prissy Pudgy Pants.'

Ah, Stella . . . so cruel, yet so amusing. 'Look, it just happened.' I recap as best I can. 'We were talking about me being a senior, prom came up, and she started carrying on about how magical it's supposed to be, but how she'll probably never get to go, since she's starting with a tutor next year.'

'Oh, Jesus,' Stella intones. 'You do realize you were set up, right?'

'No way.' I'm positive on this. 'I've heard rumors that some members of your sex can be manipulative, but Kendall? Come on. I'm telling you, we were just talking, and next thing I know I'm asking her.'

Impatiently, she snaps her gum again. 'You're such a tool,' she flatly informs me.

'Believe me, going to prom is the last thing I want to do. But it will be worth it, to have made Kendall so happy.'

Stella pulls her knees to her chin. She turns suddenly silent. Even her gum is silent. Anderlee Bennett scampers across the monitor. Someone snores in another row.

'Yo, A/B . . . ?' she says after a while.

'What?'

177

'Do people hate me?'

'Right, Stella. As if you care what anyone thinks about you.'

She punches me in the arm. 'Shut up,' she says. 'That's not true.'

If it isn't true, it's news to me.

'I've just been thinking,' she goes on. 'Ever since the video shoot. I mean, those people were horrible. They treated us like garbage, and we didn't deserve it. I wasn't expecting them to spoon-feed us caviar or anything but . . . my point is: Is that the way I treat people? Really, A/B, tell me. Because if it is, that's not good.'

How do you console someone who terrifies you? I try my best. 'You're not that bad,' I tell her. 'You're up-front and honest and you say how you feel.'

'Yeah, finish,' she demands. 'I definitely sense a "but" here . . .'

'No "but,"' I say. 'Except –'

'Ah,' she says. 'Worse than a "but." An "except."'

'Except it would go down a lot easier if you didn't make everybody eat it raw.'

She sits there for another minute, chewing my comment along with her gum. 'Yeah,' she says. 'Whatever.' And then she moves it on down the aisle.

Somewhere over the Midwest: 'Hey . . . are you sleeping? I'm sorry, I'm such a pest – I'll go . . .'

I sit up into a tickly curtain of hair. 'No, Wynn, it's cool . . .' She had jerked her head away, but on hearing me call her back moves forward. Bang – we smack foreheads. It hurts like hell, but we both laugh at low volume.

'Shit!' I hiss. 'Wynn, you all right?'

'Ouch, yeah, I guess,' she replies. 'That was funny. Painful, but funny.'

'I bet we both have goose eggs tomorrow.' I lapse into dork mode. 'That's because there are so many blood vessels in the head. To protect the brain. In fact, forget tomorrow, the welts ought to rise instantaneously . . .'

Her clothes rustle as she arranges herself next to me, legs crossed yoga-style. 'Only hickeys would be more incriminating.'

I give a little 'heh-heh-heh' and try not to dwell on *that* particular imagery. After all, ever since Wynn took a long hard look at me next-to-naked, I've been wondering how I measure up. Like if she were writing a review for hottie.com, how many stars would I rate? Plus, her seeing me in my skivvies naturally leads to thoughts about her in hers – definitely not a productive or professional place for my mind to dawdle. 'So what's going on?'

'I just want to tell you I think you're doing a wonderful thing. Really.'

'Thanks … um, what exactly is it that I'm doing?'

'Come on, I know about you taking Kendall to prom,' she says. 'And I mean it, A/B. You really are a munch.'

'Mensch,' I correct her. 'A munch is a snack – unless unless you mean Munch, that artist who did *The Scream*. But if you mean nice guy, that's mensch.' Why did the close proximity of a statuesque vanilla-scented blonde make me blather on so?

'Sorry, right: mensch.' With a pop of breath she blows her fringe from her eyes. 'I just . . . look, it's none of my business but you *have* to know Kendall has a crush on you. And maybe I'm wrong but I get the feeling you're just her friend, and a, a mensch, so you want to be nice. But seriously, A/B, you wouldn't want her to think you liked her back the way she likes you – unless you do.' Her words come at a gallop now. 'Because eventually she'll find out your true feelings don't match hers and that would be bad. Bad for Kendall, bad for you, bad for 6X. I mean, far be it from me to come off like an expert on anyone's romantic life, but unrequited love . . . it's tragic, that's all.'

Before I can respond, she sighs, unfolds herself, and pads back to her seat.

No rest for the weary. As we cross into Eastern Standard Time, an impossibly perky 'hi' assails me. Dawn light trickles into the cabin, and there's Kendall, clutching her cheapo plane pillow and blanket. 'I love flying – have I ever told you that?' she says. 'I'm not afraid to fly at all. But I really can't sleep a wink, can you?'

I am so very, very tired. Yet I have to see this trilogy to completion. I let Kendall climb over me.

'I move into the apartment this week – it is going to be so cool,' she trills. 'I'm going to have a key made for you, so you can come over whenever you like. Just I think we should keep it a secret. I wouldn't want Stella and Wynn to be jealous, but I can't be handing out keys willy-nilly. And, gosh, we simply can't let my mom know – she would not understand at all . . .'

On and on she goes, chirping like a sparrow on speed, genuinely joyful about every passing moment, until all at once she conks out, her head flopping to my shoulder. The sky grows brighter. I look at Kendall's face. She smiles as she sleeps, and the tiniest bit of drool creeps from the corner of her mouth. I watch her a bit longer, then reason it would probably be best if we land in separate rows.

I have every intention of slipping out, pulling the crummy airline blanket over her dormant form . . .

I do, I do, I swear I do.

But soon as I try, Kendall shifts her body more towards me. And she arches her back. And slits her dreamy eyes.

'A/B . . .'

The way she says my name is honey and gold and sweet summer rain . . . and something else, something I certainly can't remember ever being remotely connected to my name before. She says my name with absolute, undiluted *desire*.

Then she snuggles up closer, with her dreamy eyes and her lips still apart with my name on them.

What else can I do? I kiss her.

The Voice

Can we talk about first kisses for one little minute? A lot of first kisses probably come at a party, or on a porch, or in a car, but I don't reckon too many girls get their first kiss in an airplane. But it's not just the place – everything about this kiss is perfect and special and romantic. Of course, it's not like I know A/B is going to kiss me at all. I certainly don't throw myself at him or anything; we're simply sitting together having one of our great conversations. Then I lose track – maybe I fall asleep.

Until I feel A/B moving beside me. My eyes flutter. His face is the only thing I see; his face is my whole world. Right then I know this is it. I want him to kiss me so bad, but I don't ask him to – I couldn't do that in a million years – and yet every pump of my heart pleads: kiss me, kiss me, *kiss me*.

And he does. He gets closer and closer, and I'm almost convinced this close-enough-to-kiss-but-not-kissing is better than any kiss could be. Then he presses his lips on top of mine. Like he means to – like he *has* to. And every cell in my entire body is gossiping to its neighbour cell that this is actually going on: A/B is kissing me.

And I just . . . kiss him back. Without even knowing how, which is probably the most incredible part. It's like me and singing. No one ever taught me to do that either. It's automatic, instinctual. My arm circles his neck to hold him, my mouth opens slightly to his. It feels very intense and concentrated, yet, at the same time, scattered like stars. Shoot, I can't tell if I'm describing it right since I have nothing to compare it to. Except I will say kissing rates right up there with rock and roll and Toblerone.

Of course, I don't know what our kiss really meant. It's been more than a week, and we haven't done it again. Everything is pretty much the same, which I think is good. This girl I know, she kissed her crush at a pep rally once, and she was all bragging about it but right after that the boy got mean to her. A/B isn't being mean. There was only one awkward second as our kiss was interrupted by our captain speaking about our descent into JFK and our seat backs and tray tables being in the upright and locked position.

Ever since it's been regular. He's just good old A/B. I'm just good old Kendall. Of course, a teeny part of me is chomping at the bit, dying for more kisses. But I know it's a good thing to take it slow. So I think about our kiss – and how it will make prom night so much more special.

Only one thing has changed. Now there is music inside me. Usually, I hear songs all around me – birds, people talking, traffic on a city street. I am simply one of those people who hears a symphony in ordinary things – but it's always outside of me. Now there is a song *inside* of me. A melody magically created with my first kiss, it's purer and sweeter than any song I've ever known.

183

The Boy

McManus gives me a nod, holds the door. At least, I think he's McManus. The Teen Towers is crawling with uniforms; it's hard to keep them straight. Kendall only moved in a couple weeks ago and I haven't been there that many times, yet they all seem to know me. I wonder what Kendall told them…

'Tonight's the big night, eh?' McManus or whoever asks.

I lift the plastic suit bag encasing my rented tuxedo. 'Yep,' I say and scoot into the lift.

Ah, 14G. My new home away from home, my secret lair, my pied-à-terre. It's quite a sweet setup. True to the Teen Towers tag, Kendall's furnished apartment is decidedly kid-friendly. Plushy couch and some beanbag chairs, ample entertainment centre, colourful area rugs protecting hardwood floors from the spillage that management no doubt expects. It's a rectangular space with a capsule kitchen and a Murphy bed. That Murphy, what a brainiac. Pull a handle on the wall and – ta-da: bed. Don't need it anymore? Presto: It disappears back into the wall.

That's a beautiful thing. Me plus Kendall plus couch is

temptation enough; a bed out in the middle of everything could be too much. So far there's been no repeat of our mile-high mini-makeout, and I'm avoiding the issue since I don't have a clue how I want things to proceed. And now it's prom night, Kendall is my date, and she's supposed to meet me here in two hours. Hoping to get my mind off the 'relationship' entirely, I head for the terrace to smoke a bowl. Alas, this has the reverse affect. Instead of chilling me out, I obsess.

I even made a list. Here, look – I'll read it.

Plus side:

1) Kendall behaves as though I invented oxygen.
2) Having a girlfriend in my band would be extremely convenient.
3) I do actually like her. You know, sort of.

Minus side:

1) Kendall is Christian. Between the inevitable proselytizing and blue balls, a guy could go nuts.
2) Having an ex-girlfriend in my band would be extremely inconvenient.
3) The specter of Stella's disapproval makes me break out in hives.

Stalemate. Screw it. I go inside and shower, scrunch product into my hair, and sit around staring at the tube in my skivvies.

I wish I'd brought a guitar with me; I can't watch *TV* without noodling. Five o'clock rolls around – time to put on the monkey suit.

Thankfully, my date has agreed to certain compromises in the prom experience, which I've proposed as either practical or ironic.

1. We'll skip the limo. Kendall still technically resides in Jersey, I live on the Island, and the prom is on Central Park South (my hoity-toity high school wouldn't dream of having its denouement dance anyplace but a Manhattan hotel). Ergo, a luxury ride would be insane on so many levels. Besides, to rock stars such as we, limousines are no big whoop – but won't it be wacky fun to take the subway all dressed up.

2. We'll also pass on the pre-prom photo-op in some friend's backyard. Another geographical nightmare. Plus, I only have one real friend attending anyway: Dave Blume, my former Rosemary's Plankton bandmate.

The plan is for Kendall to primp in New Jersey, drive in with her mom, then let Mrs Taylor snap pictures before we hop the train to meet Dave, his date, and some other people for a pre-prom dinner. This is one part of the ritual I could not talk Kendall out of. And I didn't even try convincing her to forgo the flowers.

Shit, the flowers. Lickety-split, I remove all evidence of my presence from the apartment and leave to get Kendall's corsage. Then I'll cool my heels till six-thirty, when I can safely return to the Teen Towers and knock on the door to pick her up. That's our plot, our conspiracy – Mrs Taylor must never know I have keys to the crib.

The Voice

The Long Island accent is harsh and nasal and not very pretty at all. So on prom night, when I float into the restroom to freshen up after dancing with A/B, it's not exactly music to my ears.

'So you're with *Fart*elberg?'

This girl is daubing clear gloss on her lips with a pinkie as she speaks, so I can barely understand her. 'Excuse me?' I ask.

She smushes her lips together and smiles at me, but it's the girl beside her at the marble bank of bathroom sinks who repeats, real slow: 'Fart . . . el . . . berg. You're . . . with . . . *Fart* . . . el . . . berg . . .'

I wonder if they're sisters. Their dresses are so similar – plain, black, above the knee (what Wynn calls 'cocktail length'). Shiny and stick-straight, their long dark hair is scattered with identical cinnamon flecks. One girl has small, close-set eyes and full lips, the other has large, wide eyes and thin lips, but they have the exact same nose. They're also very slim, and have matching, even suntans.

'Maybe she doesn't know her date's name,' the first girl says, scrutinizing her eyebrows in the mirror.

'Oh – you mean A/B.' I'm glad to know what the heck they're talking about.

Now I get it. They're making fun of A/B, and it's hurtful to me, but I'm obliged to turn the other cheek; I just look at my hands as I soap them up and rinse them off.

'So is he your boyfriend?'

Glancing at the girls, I notice that one is slightly taller. This question comes from the taller one.

'Oh . . .' I ponder on this. I don't really know the answer, and even if I did I don't know if I'd want to tell them. 'You know, we're in this band together . . .'

'Oh, right,' says the slightly shorter one. 'You're one of those band girls.'

'That's right – we saw you on MTV,' says Miss Taller. 'That's quite an . . . *interesting* hairdo you've got in the video.'

'Yes,' says her friend. 'It's really *interesting* . . .'

'How come you're not wearing your hair like that tonight?'

I am toweling off my hands, wondering how to politely make an exit. These girls are being rude, but I won't stoop to their level. 'That hairstyle? It was part of the concept. The stylist created it especially for me – for the video,' I explain. 'My mom did my hair for prom.'

The way they bust up, this is the funniest thing they've heard in all their born days.

'Your *mom!*'

'How *Sweet!*'

I check my hair in the mirror – my mom did it nice. I try to throw my towel in the trash, but now the girls are blocking my way.

'Excuse me . . .' I say.

'No, excuse me,' says Miss Shorter. 'I just want to ask you a question. See, we heard that your band got signed because your drummer hooked up with some executive from the record company.'

'Specifically, we heard she sucked him off,' says the other one.

I drop my towel on the sink. I wish I could think of some way to put these girls in their place, but now they're being crude as well as rude, and I do not know how to deal with that kind of talk.

Anyway, that's not what we really want to know,' the girl continues. 'We're just dying to know about all the nasty stuff between you and Fartelberg. So tell us – do you suck him off? Do you?'

My mouth is open but nothing's coming out. Just the very idea of taking something as pure and decent as my love for A/B and tainting it with . . . with . . . oh my gosh, I cannot bear it!

A veil of red falls over my eyes. My feet, hands, and forehead prickle and sting. I don't know how I find my way back to the table, but once I get there I don't even have one second to get my composure back. The MC is calling my name. Everyone at A/B's table is standing and staring at me. A/B grabs me by the elbow.

'Come on . . .' He leans into my ear. 'They want you to sing. Come on . . .'

Sing? Faint is more likely. Yet one foot lands in front of the other somehow. And here is the stage. One, two, three steps. If only the floor would open up and swallow me.

And all at once something snaps. I tap into the voice within the voice, and I am illuminated. I am righteous. The stinging and prickling have sparked a conflagration. I seize the mike stand like a sword.

'What is it, babe?' the MC asks me. 'What do you want to do?'

I name the song, and he tells the lead guitarist. Of course, he knows it. Bands that play proms and weddings, they need a big repertoire. Besides, it was such a hit a while back. Way before 6X, I sang it at a pageant; I still know all the words by heart. The guitarist nods, but I pull on his cuff – I have to tell him the tempo. He gives me a look as if to make sure I'm sure, but I'm sure. I'm very sure.

'This one goes out to all you Queens of Sheba,' I say into the mike. 'Consider it your wake-up call…'

Initially, no one recognizes what I'm singing. They know it as a pop ballad, overripe with strings. I'm ripping it apart and putting it back together with the purity of my wrath; I'm taking it on, making it mine, and by the time I kick into the chorus – 'I am beautiful, no matter what they say . . .' – the ballroom is one big mosh pit.

A squeal of feedback bangs the ceiling, falls back on the crowd like icy hail. Fittingly, the applause is like thunder, but I couldn't care less. To be gracious, I give a little bow, but the way I square my shoulders and toss back my head with a terse, sharp 'thank you' conveys exactly how I feel. I am done here. A/B meets me at the stairs; he's hugging me, lifting me off my feet. Sweaty kids in expensive clothes mob me, telling me how awesome I am and how they can't wait to get our album when it comes out. A/B has his arm around my shoulders, helping me make my way.

It takes forever to cross the dance floor; once we're back at our table it's nearly my curfew. We'll have to hustle to get me home on the dot. I'm a little sad that we won't have any time alone, but as A/B whisks me out the door and into the warm night air, I feel wonderful and powerful and, yes, beautiful, just like the song says.

The Boss

Want to know what's good about a fancy-ass school where kids are constantly taking off to visit their actor parents on location? Nobody blinks an eye when you say you gotta be out for a few days here and there to cut a record. Only forget Hit Factory. We're making the album at Broken Sound. It's more low-key (aka cheaper), but I'm cool with it. That slick Hit Factory vibe is so not us. Plus, Slushie says big studios reek with the sweat of vanity and greed.

He's our producer . . . so far. At least he'll work with us on our covers. The big purple elephant in the room no one wants to talk about is original material – that is, our lack thereof. The label keeps sending us demos from different songwriter-producers. You'd think we'd be eager to discuss them at our next band meeting. But no. Here's the conversation, verbatim:

Wynn: Come on, spill. Details, please. Don't leave anything out.

A/B: Well, first of all, Kendall looked beautiful.

Kendall: Oh, now, you're such a liar. You know I was only wearing that same old dress I wore to the premiere.

Wynn: I bet you looked gorgeous. Something about prom night gives a girl that extra edge. How did the dinner go?

Kendall: I was a little nervous meeting A/B's friends –

A/B: Correction: friend.

Kendall: I don't know why you say that – everyone seems to like you. And they were all nice to me. Plus, Wynn, that restaurant you suggested was perfect. Very elegant.

A/B: Yeah, the most elegant part was when Josh Klein shoved a shrimp up his nose.

Me (beginning to lose my shit): What did this loser do for an encore? Mainline steak sauce?

Wynn: So come on, get to the prom . . .

Kendall: Well, that hotel is like a palace, like some place you'd see in Europe. The ballroom was straight out of Cinderella.

Wynn: Did you dance?

Kendall: Yes –

A/B: No –

A/B and Kendall: Tee-hee-hee-hee . . .

Kendall: Well, we shuffled around the floor a few times – I think that counts.

A/B: But wait, the best part was when the MC announced that Kendall Taylor was in the house, and he called her to the stage for a song . . .

Are you ready to vomit yet? I'm getting the dry heaves here sharing it. Once Kendall finishes describing some chick's pedicure, the subject is finally exhausted and we get down to business. We talk about the songs, and there's one thing we definitely agree on: They all suck.

'Well, isn't that just too bad,' I say. 'We're sitting here, crybabying, while the label wants a taste of new stuff. And they're not gonna wait forever.'

'Stella's right,' says A/B. 'Gaylord promised them we'd have a rough track of *something* by next week.'

Kendall waves her hand. 'You know me, I can sing anything.' Oh, she's just so accommodating I could strangle her.

'I don't know . . .' Wynn nibbles her fingernails. 'If we just record some random song, it's going to show that our hearts aren't in it. I'd rather not give Preston anything than a go-through-the-motions track.'

Our waitress leaves a bill on the table, and I throw down some cash. 'We gotta feel it, all right, but sometimes you gotta force it,' I say. 'Look, we're supposed to be at Broken in fifteen minutes. So how 'bout this: We pick a tune, any tune, and slog through it. That way, when Preston and them complain we can turn it around and say it's not our fault they picked shitty songwriters.'

Nobody is crazy about the idea. But, excuse me: At least I have one.

The Body

What a disaster. Stella tries to rally us, but we're dragging our feet the whole way to Broken and then we just procrastinate. I swear, A/B has to rearrange his stomp pedals eighteen times. Alan Slushinger is getting itchy, twirling his hair. I feel bad, but I cannot get it up for any of these songs. None of us can.

It's not that they're bad; they're just not us. *Happy Lies* is energetic, and Alan helps me figure out a beefy way to play it, but the lyrics are insipid, what some twenty-something thinks kids care about. And *Dolly* is a cool punk rock song, but a waste of Kendall's range; it's basically a chord and a half, no melody at all. There's another one, it doesn't even have a name, just *Potential 6X Anthem*, but that's retarded – you have to *believe* an anthem. It's different with our covers – they've been established by other artists but we completely reinterpret them. These new tunes are ostensibly tailor-made for us, but they so do not fit.

I keep stealing glances at Stella – she's got to share my frustration. It's different for A/B and Kendall; they don't struggle like we do. For us, it's tough enough to learn any song, but a song written for you by people who don't know you, a song whose soul is fake . . . not fun. I'd reach out to her, but her impatience is toxic. Slushie tells her 'try this' or 'try that' and she just mimics him. Or she glowers at Kendall, who spends most of her time in the Lay-Z-Boy scarfing M&M's or making moony eyes at A/B.

Well, Stella may have the shortest fuse, but I know it won't be long till we're all snapping each other's heads off. Alan can sense it too; he tells us to take a break.

And that's when the miracle begins to unfold.

The Boy

I have gotten heavily into coffee lately. Not just drinking it, fixing it. That's how it is with guys. Put us in action hero pyjamas as little kids and we're action hero wannabes for the rest of our lives. When there's a problem, we want to fix it, and if we can't fix it, we fix something else. Say, coffee.

The problem at hand: serious musical dysfunction. Every fibre of my being believes I should be able to correct this – concoct an arrangement or lay down a lick that makes any tune feel and sound 6X. And I try. But I fail. So I fix coffee.

The machine in the Broken Sound kitchenette is my new best friend – now that I've carefully, lovingly, cleaned it top to bottom with distilled vinegar. I buy gourmet beans (a blend of Kona and Colombian) and, after various experiments, have gotten the grind just right. Naturally, I prefer it be drunk black; I get visibly upset if you taint it with more than a dollop of half-and-half. Slushie and Wynn water it down with so much semi-skimmed milk I could cry. Kendall's cup is mostly sugar and half-and-half, yet even then she's pretending to like it. Stella's the only true aficionado. Which makes her dependent on me. Which, perversely enough, I enjoy.

'So, who wants some joe?' I rub my hands together briskly after we turn in another miserable rendition of *Dolly*. 'I know I do.' I place my guitar on its stand.

'Yeah, sure, why not,' says Stella.

Since I've had three cups already, I make a piss-stop before getting with my beloved brew pot. When I reach the kitchenette, I find Kendall with her head in the fridge.

And she's humming.

'Wow, what's that?' I ask her.

She straightens up quickly and turns to me. Does she think I was ogling her ass?

'Oh! Hi!' she says. 'What's what?'

'That thing . . . that song.' She stares at me like a droid with a loose wire.

'You know, that thing you're humming.'

Suddenly she turns crimson, yet she's smiling too, but trying not to, so basically she resembles a ripe tomato with a nervous tic. 'Oh, that . . .'

'That indeed,' I say. 'Is it one of the demos?'

'Oh gosh . . . no . . .' she says, hedging.

'Because I don't remember it. And if I'd heard it I'd definitely remember – it's beautiful.'

'It is?' she asks.

'Yeah . . . so what is it?'

Trailing her fingers on the kitchen counter, she says, almost guiltily, 'It's mine.'

'What do you mean, it's yours?' I'm flabbergasted. 'You *wrote* it?'

Kendall shakes her head, examines her feet. 'It just came to

199

me.' She raises her eyes. 'It's been going around and around in my head . . . since . . . the *plane*.'

The plane? I think. 'The plane?' I say.

She dips her eyes again.

'Oh . . . the *plane*.' I get it now. 'Wow, really? You mean after we . . . ?'

She looks at me, simultaneously giddy and sober. 'Yep . . .'

'Wow . . .'

'Yep . . .'

I take one giant step closer to her. She backs up against the counter.

'Wow, that's . . . that's amazing.'

'So what's the deal on that coffee?' Stella storms in, empty mug in hand.

She can't break the spell, though. 'Do it again,' I tell Kendall. 'Do it for Stella.'

'What's going on in here?' Stella wants to know. 'Is there coffee or what?'

'Shhh, Stella.' I can't believe I actually shush her. 'Listen to this. Kendall, don't hum it, la-la-la it.'

And she does. And damn if it doesn't shut Stella up.

'That's pretty.' She forgets all about her caffeine fix. 'Almost too pretty.'

'Yeah,' I concur. 'But if we transpose it. Wait a second . . .'

I race off to get my guitar, but they follow me towards the studio instead – I hear Kendall's bare-bones explanation that the melody 'just came' to her. I strike a chord. 'See, there's nothing sadder than A minor,' I say. 'So when you take something super-pretty and put it in that key . . .' I pluck Kendall's melody from memory.

'It changes it up,' marvels Stella. 'Gives it an edge.'

'Hey . . .' Wynn joins us. 'Where'd you get that?'

'I made it up,' Kendall says, comfortable with the idea now. She la-la-las it again as I play.

'And the bass line could be all sludgy,' suggests Stella. 'To add weight.'

'I could sing it lower too . . .' offers Kendall. 'Knock it down an octave.'

We start jamming on that hint of a hook just to see where it takes us. Next thing we know, we've got a chorus. Slushie walks in and stands there with his hands clasped in front of him, his expression approving and weirdly knowing.

Then it all comes to a crashing halt. Kendall quits singing.

'What's wrong?' I ask her. 'Why'd you stop?'

She sighs. 'Because it's silly,' she says. 'Gosh, I don't want to be a party pooper; I love my little melody and all. But what is it? What can we call it: "Something in A Minor"? I can't just go la-la-la for an entire song.'

She's right, of course. We are so screwed.

'Oh well.' I take off my guitar. 'Guess I'll go see about that coffee.'

'Wait . . .' says Wynn, very softly. 'A/B, you guys, wait.' Her voice is surer now, committed. 'Let me get my journal . . .'

The Boss

What did I say? No, really, what did I tell you? Behind the silver-platter profile and that too-shy-to-try smile pumps the soul of a poet. My girl Wynn is a warrior princess of words – and she is popping. Who cares that she's been hiding it, letting us think there's nothing in her notebook but typical teen confessions. That damn journal is crammed with lyrics: funny songs, sad songs, how-can-life-be-so-incomprehensibly-stupid songs.

Kendall may have come in with a couple of tra-la-las, but don't get it twisted: Wynn's the one who's turning 6X into bona fide songwriters. We've got three already, and we sent Preston Schenk a rough version of *All Over Oliver* – formerly known as *Something in A Minor*. The label is loving it, all right. They're talking single. But they ain't heard nothing yet. *Oliver* is catchy and relatable – it's about this girl who hooks up with her crush, then finds out he went after her because his boys dared him to. Bubblegum angst, we call it. It's cool, but wait till we lay down *Lingerie Model*, which Wynn is gonna sing, and *Bliss de la Mess*, my personal favourite.

Brian's tripping over this new development, but that's not

keeping him from lawyer mode. He set up HotShit Music to get our publishing straight – royalties and things like that. Let's be clear: Wynn gets extra – she writes the words. But the music is by all of us, since we all contribute our parts.

If you ask me, Kendall doesn't do a damn thing creatively. Granted, she burped up the hook for *Oliver*, but A/B took it from there, and he's also the musical force behind *Lingerie Model* and *Bliss*. Basically, Kendall shows up and sings as needed. This week she's doing her vocals and video gig for that Windows by Gina tune, so she's hardly around at all. And guess what? That suits me fine.

The Body

I'm walking down Second Avenue today and this car pulls up to a light, Alice Cooper's *School's Out* blasting from the speakers. This old guy with a ponytail is smacking the steering wheel and screaming along, oblivious to everyone. The song's a bit premature – there's still one more full week of classes left – but I so know where he's coming from.

I'm really looking forward to summer, even though we'll be working our butts off. Baring my soul as 6X's lyricist isn't exactly easy either, but everyone's treating me like I'm Dylan Thomas or Bob Dylan or somebody – very supportive. One cool thing about doing our own stuff is Alan Slushinger is officially aboard full-time. Those demos we'd been getting all came from different songwriter-producer teams; if we went with a bunch, we'd have to install a revolving door in the studio. It feels more natural to work with one person you know and trust. We adore Alan, and he's such a tunesmith himself – he helps us out when we get stuck.

The songwriting process is awesome. My stupid scribbles will inspire A/B to crank out a couple of chords, or Stella will pick up on the cadence, or Kendall will just start wailing and …

it happens. Plus, it's improving our group dynamic. (OK, Stella still considers Kendall a synonym for plague, but she appears to be rechanneling her nastier urges. And Kendall must be crushing so hard on A/B she doesn't seem to care.)

The way we operate now is, if the muse is with us, we write and lay down scratch tracks; if not, we record our covers. Chances are, *You're All I've Got . . . Teenage FBI*, and *The Waiting* – and *Dirty Boots*, of course – will all be on our debut. Losing those tunes would be like cutting off a limb.

So it'll be two months of sweaty, sticky, smelly New York City and the four-wall confines of Broken Sound for us. Glamorous? Not too. But it beats camp. I hate camp. Nature, the woods, laying out by the lake – fine. But summer camp is mostly an excuse for horny kids to hook up in the dark. My two make-outs took place at camp last year. Ick. Not that I can pinpoint exactly what was so icky about it – both guys had been exceptionally cute. Mr July was a lacrosse sensation with a golden tan, golden close-cropped curls, very all-American and smelling like grass. Mr August was his polar opposite – a pale, jaded CIT who smoked Silk Cut cigarettes and never removed his sunglasses (even with his tongue down my throat); he couldn't fathom how his parents managed to con him into anything as bourgeois as summer camp.

Believe me, this absence of ardour for either guy had me very perplexed. At night, I'd lie in my bunk and listen to my cabinmates squeal on and on over this or that boy's kiss, and I'd think, *How come I'm not feeling it?* Once I was back home and away from the constant scrutiny of bunk life, I decided to figure it out. Like a science project. Like a self-improvement plan. I bought a copy of *Cosmo* – that magazine always has at least six articles on orgasm per issue. 'Pleasure *Yourself* to Drive *Him* Wild!' is the type of journalistic excellence I'm talking about.

Well, I read the story and then got down to business with a torch and hand mirror. Hello, clitoris – aren't you cute! It was all very technical; I learned a lot about anatomy. I put the mirror away, leaned back on some pillows, and began to touch myself. Really concentrated on what I was doing – but to no avail. And I swear I was not a quitter on this score; I kept at it on a nightly basis. And I tried everything. Firm strokes, feathery strokes, fluttery strokes. I mean I was committed to coming. And it was pleasurable – it felt good. Until it started to get irritating. And frustrating. I just couldn't get over the hump. After a month of diligent masturbatory experiments, I became convinced: Regardless of having all the right parts in all the right places, there was definitely something wrong with me.

The Voice

Tomorrow, A/B will be a high-school graduate. He's not looking forward to the ceremony, marching down the aisle to what he calls *Puke and Circumstance*, but he's going anyway to please his parents. He didn't invite me, and I kind of wish he had, but graduation is about family, and family is sacred. Still, I sure am proud of him.

But I'm also feeling somewhat out of sorts. A little lonely, disconnected. Shuttling back and forth between New Jersey and the Teen Towers. Knowing that come September, I won't be in regular high school anymore – and wondering how I'll stay in touch with the Taras and my other friends. Of course, it's awfully exciting and just so grown-up doing *Wonder Bread* with Windows by Gina, being in the video and all. The concept is so cool: There's a trampoline shaped like a loaf of bread, and I get to bounce up and down on it. Plus, the people at that video shoot? They're much nicer to me than the people on *Dirty Boots*. Yet I had this tickle in my tummy the whole time – I'm not in Windows by Gina, I'm not part of the crew, I'm … floating.

As to 6X, things are just wonderful with us writing our own

songs. Wynn is such a talented lyricist. Some of her lines are not my type of language. Like when the girl in *All Over Oliver* goes on about doing the deed. My inner rock chick has to work overtime on that one or the words would stick in my craw. Mostly, though, I like singing what Wynn writes. She sure can cut straight to the every-girl essence of the thing. Sometimes she's blunt, sometimes she's coy, but by the time the song is done you cannot help but think, *Yes, that's exactly how I feel*. She puts it just right – and it rhymes too. It's funny, I can be a real chatterbox and just chew your ear off, but when it comes to writing, words are a giant log jam. So I admire Wynn a lot. It's only that the focus has shifted off me some; I'm not so much the star anymore. Not that it bothers me one little bit.

Besides, our fans still see me as the main attraction. Just look at the 6X website. I plunked down a bunch of my deal money on a new laptop (my mom agreed, since our old home computer was so dinky, and I'll need something high-tech come next term, for working with my tutor). Ever since I bought it, I've been spending tons of time on our site, and I get the most fan mail. The way it's set up, people can contact each band member directly, and it's like the whole world is reaching out to me. Lots of girls see me as a role model. But I have boy fans too.

In fact, I've been getting a heap of mail from this one guy. I think he may have a crush on me. He writes the nicest e-mails – always full of flattery. And the way he words things . . . it's almost like he knows me. I think about him quite a bit – especially when A/B falls into one of his spells. A/B can fixate on a chord progression to the exclusion of everything (and everyone) else, like it's a coded message from the Lord Almighty.

I've been waiting and waiting for A/B to kiss me again. He gets so caught up in everything else that's going on; sometimes I think he takes me for granted. But it's good that A/B is a gentleman – he has way too much respect for me to paw at me on the couch whenever we're alone. That's one of the reasons I'm falling in love with him.

So it's easy for my mind to just amble over to my superfan. Although the only thing I really know about him is his screen name. He calls himself CountryBoy.

The Body

'**W**ow, Kendall, this is . . .'

I want to say this is crazy, I want to say this is creepy, I want to say this is actually kind of gross. I wish I could stick with the political feminist poetry lying open in my lap, but my IQ has apparently plummeted to negative 20 – I can't make heads or tails of Adrienne Rich. As Kendall shuffles papers next to me on the Boston Shuttle, en route to a show – punctuating her shuffles with murmured my-oh-mys – I take the bait and shut my book to suss out the source of her muted squeals. The way she protests, you'd think she was reviewing classified documents. Ultimately, though, she swears me to secrecy and foists these printouts on me. Three seconds later I realize her reading comprehension is challenged too. The messages make my ick meter tick like mad.

'This is . . . intense.' It's the best I can do. Kendall's all lit up over this stack of fan mail, and I can't bear to pull the plug.

'It is.' She swivels her head to check for KGB. 'The first few, I felt, well, isn't that nice. But now . . . it seems like he's obsessed with me. I don't encourage him, of course – that wouldn't be fair to A/B.'

Obsessed is right. You could choke on this CountryBoy's infatuated fawning:

Dear Kendall, From the moment I saw you on MTV I knew you were something special. I love how you sing. I bet you always sang that pretty, ever since you was a baby. When I hear your voice you brighten up my whole world. And you seem so real! Like lots of those girls on MTV are fake and skinny but you don't need to be that way. You are a natrul star!

Hey little lady! Saw your video again and just had to write. Cause I can't get enough of you. I was mad when I went down to by that Steal This Pony soundtrack and you only had one song on it. Tell me – are you going to have an album of your own? I would by that one in a heartbeat. I could listen to you sing day and night. Something about your voice touches me like nothing else.

Hey Angel, its me. I sure wish you'd write me back one day. The webside says these letters go strait to you personal, and I know your a busy lady but it would make me feel so good to hear from you. Not just because your a famous star and so pretty. Heres the reason why. When I see you sing, your with your band – but your apart from them too. That is how I feel in this life sometimes. Like even tho theres people around – friends and girls and all – I am alone.

Maybe I'm paranoid. Or evil . . . envious. My inbox on the 6X site isn't exactly a barren black hole, but I don't get nearly as much fan mail as Kendall. Maybe I'm wishing someone would ooze all over me. No, jealousy wouldn't cause the uh-oh vibe I'm getting from Kendall's superfan. It has nothing to do with his second-grade literacy level either . . . I'm not a snob like that.

I can't help it. I feel it in my bones. This CountryBoy spells T-R-U-B-B-L-E.

The Boss

Forget freak of the week; Kendall Taylor is the freak of the century. Yeah, we're all a little on edge since tonight we're gonna play *All Over Oliver* live for the first time. I've got a mutha of a pimple on my chin. And A/B has a cold – he's being such a baby. Guys are like that when they're sick, they need their mommies, but his dad's along on the Boston trip and Mr F. the elder is useless. Clearly, the man has never heard of Benalin.

Plus, the club is a complete hole. The bathroom hasn't been cleaned since Jessica Simpson wore a training bra. Sound check? More like shit check – the PA must be busted or something. Anyway, we're running through *All Over Oliver*, and Kendall goes into this whirl when – *snap!* The heel on her boot breaks, and she lands smack on her ass. 'Waaahh!' she starts bawling. We all rush over. What if she sprained an ankle – that would suck. But she's fine. No broken bones, no ambulance required.

Yet the baby will not calm down. It's diva time.

'This cannot be happening!' she cries. 'I cannot go on tonight!'

'Ooh, Kendall, it's OK, don't worry,' Wynn tells her soothingly.

A/B and his dad have her by the elbows, but she wrenches away. 'It is not OK!' she shrieks. 'Don't tell me it's OK, Wynn Morgan. You don't know anything.' Still wailing, she hobbles off the stage – *ka-clunk, kaclunk* – and sits at a table, burying her head in her arms. Everyone follows like her freakin' entourage.

'Sorry, Kendall – you're right, we don't know,' says Wynn, aka the white Oprah Winfrey. 'Come on, tell us. What's going on, what's wrong?'

Kendall blubbers. Wynn flicks a glance at A/B and his dad that says, *Step off; this is a chick thing.* They are all too relieved to recede. Then Wynn looks beseechingly at me, as if I know what to do – I bug my eyes at her but her eyes beg back: *please.* I pull out a chair and we sit on either side of this southern-fried fruitcake.

All puffy and pig-eyed, she lifts her head. 'The only other shoes I have with me are . . . are . . . *sneakers.*'

'Yeah?' Look, I am trying to be sensitive but I do not get it. 'So?'

'I cannot sing in *sneakers* . . .' A fresh round of sobs.

'Ooh-shh, ooh-shh,' Wynn makes comforting coos. 'You can borrow my shoes.'

'Noooo!' A siren howls out of her. 'You only wear *flaaaaats.*'

Of course. I'm catching on now. So should Wynn, since we've both seen it countless times: Kendall's regular Captain Quirk about footwear – her high-heel fetish is no joke. Two solutions occur to me.

'Kendall, if you would kindly shut up, we can deal with this,'

I tell her. 'We can A) find a shoemaker in this town and get your boot fixed. Or B) if we leave right now you can buy yourself a new pair of heels, which is my recommendation because hello, it's practically summer and you're still stuffing your tootsies into boots.'

Kendall sniffs. Wynn looks at me like she could nominate me for the Nobel Prize.

'Maybe some pretty sandals?' Wynn coaxes. 'Would you like that?'

Kendall wipes her face with her sleeve. 'Yes,' she says, 'that would be cool . . .'

So Wynn hits up the barmaid for shopping suggestions and instead of chilling at the hotel, the two of us go with Whack Job for a new pair of show shoes.

If only all problems could be solved so easily.

The Boy

The Boston gig is a fiasco. Not because we play bad – in fact, we play great . . . to approximately three people. See, Boston's a huge college town, but school let out a few weeks ago and what human being with a fake or bona fide ID can resist when the barstool sand beaches of Cape Cod and the Vineyard beckon? As to the high-school set, yes, our show at The Rat is all ages. But it's also the same night as the local 'hot' radio station's Summer Spank concert. Every kid with the price of admission is headed to see the likes of Ludacris and Good Charlotte and Angel Blue do two songs apiece.

But the show must go on, right? In my mind, this gig is basically a practice at a crummy club in a city where the pizza sucks. I'm all for catching the shuttle home afterwards, but we have promo bits at two radio stations tomorrow – including the same 'hot' station that didn't ask us to their Summer Spank. I'd throw a tantrum if I weren't a fountain of snot. To add insult to injury, my father is along for the ride. Here, in the shadow of Harvard. Not his alma mater – he wishes. He's not saying a word; he's hoping I will breathe the air of Cambridge and come to my higher-learning senses.

Except the joke's on him: Right now I'm so congested I can't breathe.

My dad wrote the book on passive-aggressive. The way he's *kvelling* over Wynn, with her slim volume of arcane poetry. And Stella, the two of them yammering away in Spanish, him swooning over her conjugation and telling her she really ought to tackle Italian next. Sheesh. Parents with high expectations should have a lot of kids. Better their odds that they'll get what they want. Only children have it tough – who can handle the pressure?

And of course we're sharing a hotel room (bunking with the designated parent is part of our economy plan), which means listening to Dad's snores of disappointment all night. As he showers, I contemplate tying an anvil to my foot and throwing myself into the Charles River. When the phone starts ringing, I'm so deeply entrenched in this fugue state I think I'll just let it. But I can't resist; I grab it before it stops.

'Get over to Wynn's room, *stat*.' It's Stella.

'What for?' I whine. 'I don't feel good. I think I have a temperature . . .'

She spits the room number and hangs up harshly.

I obey.

And I am not sorry.

'Heyyyy! Now we can really get this party started.' I am yanked inside by . . . which one is it – Evangeline or Epiphany? Hard to say; things start to get real fuzzy real fast. Evangeline's the barmaid from The Rat, Epiphany's her partner in crime – we refer to them simply as the E Girls – E1 and E2. Both are prime examples of a certain breed. Age? Somewhere between legal and retirement. Tattooed. Pierced. Built like they leaped out of the Final Fantasy series. Indisputably hot. And they come bearing substances: Two quarts of Jack Daniels and a ball of hash the size of a gob-stopper – the room's already hazy and stanky from puffs on the pipe.

Wynn and Stella are there too, of course. The shindig's roots lie in Wynn speed-bonding with E1 in The Rat restroom – something about a bunny tattoo being the cutest thing ever. E1 invites herself back to the hotel; E2 comes out of a stall and wants in.

'We've never done it with kids before,' E1 says now.

'Done what?' says Wynn.

E1 and E2 laugh like twin tambourines. 'Partied, of course,' says E2, who adds that she wants to do the girls' hair. Not that she's a professional stylist; she's more of a hair savant.

Whatever, it's a go . . .

E1 flicks a lighter as Wynn sucks down a wicked hit. She can barely hold it, giggling on the exhalation. Stella has a toke, breathes out slowly and deliciously, then starts jumping on the bed.

'That TV set better be bolted down,' she hollers, 'or it's going out the freakin' window.'

Then she charges at me, just as E1 is giving me fire, and slaps me on the back, which makes me choke on the smoke and look like a novice in front of the E Girls.

'What do you think, A/B?' Stella says. 'Should we ask Kendall to pop in?'

'Damn straight,' says E1. 'Gotta have the lead singer.'

'Yeah, she's adorable,' says E2. 'I'd like to get my hands on her head too.'

OK, Stella's kidding – but Kendall is a rock chick in training, and the E Girls have advanced degrees in the subject. So much to everyone's surprise, I chug a few swigs of Jack and pick up the phone.

The Voice

It's taken me forever to fall asleep – for some reason, the later I stay up, the harder it is to conk out – and when the phone rings I get all flustered, figuring it must be morning and I'm late for the radio station. My heart is beating a mile a minute as I grope for the receiver. There's so much calamity going on in the background, it's hard to hear who's on the line. But it's not the hotel operator with my wake-up call.

It's A/B.

My heart continues pounding – for a different reason. When your crush calls as you lay alone in a strange bed in a strange city . . . well, it is awfully romantic. Maybe he's been tossing and turning, tortured with emotion – he needs to speak to me so bad.

But no. He's shouting that I should come to Wynn's room for a party.

Well, I am in my PJs. My teeth are brushed. And quite frankly after being with my bandmates all day and half the night, I've had my fill of those girls. I am trying to find a nice way to say this so that no one gets offended when A/B yells above the din, 'Come on, Kendall! Evangeline and Epiphany are dying to meet you.'

Abruptly my heart goes from fluttering to what feels like a stone-cold stop. I actually remove the phone from my ear to stare at it in disbelief by the strand of light seeping through the cracked bathroom door. A/B is not merely out late with Wynn and Stella, but two other girls as well. And he expects me to join them? I never! The code by which I was raised is deeply ingrained in me: A lady does not jump when a boy calls; she certainly does not dash out of bed in the middle of the night and jockey for position with a legion of other females.

Don't think for a moment that this is some quaint, old-fashioned notion; nosiree, just the opposite. My mom is a strong, independent career woman who taught me never to permit some man to run my life or lure me into straying from what is right. She never has and never will. My daddy treated her with utmost respect and after he was called to Jesus, she remained true to his memory rather than settle for less.

While I wonder how to convey this very vital information in no uncertain terms, I hear A/B cry, 'Ouch!' followed by the crash of the phone hitting a piece of furniture or something. I should hang up that very second but the horrible rumpus has my ears bewitched – a herd of elephants and a flock of magpies are square-dancing in there, stomping, trumpeting, squawking, shrieking.

Finally, A/B gets back on the phone. 'Kendall? You still there? Sorry about that. So you coming? Come on!'

'No, A/B, *I'm* sorry,' I tell him. 'But I have no interest in partying with a pack of wild animals. Good night!' I slam the receiver so hard it vibrates in my hand. Then I fluff the pillows and rearrange the blankets and flip from my stomach to my side to my back but I cannot for the life of me get back to sleep because I am just so mad. So I lay in that long, wide hotel bed until dawn courts the curtains.

Then I throw some clothes on and head to the hotel coffee shop for pancakes, sausage, and eggs. No, I do *not* want any coffee.

When I am done with breakfast I march over to reception to find out if there is a computer available to guests – I had to pack light and left my laptop at home. The woman behind the desk does not dare give me that oh-you-pesky-teenager look. She tells me helpfully that the hotel has a fully equipped business office at my disposal. I go straight there and log on to the Internet.

Dear CountryBoy . . .

For once, when I write, the words pour out of me like water over rocks.

The Boss

Rock and roll is my life, but if I had to do something else? Anthropology. Poking into how culture determines destiny, that's interesting to me. Too bad there's no money in it. Let's call it my new hobby. Nurture versus nature and that shit. Why is Kendall such a nutcase: Is it her brain or how she was brought up? What makes Wynn so passive – biology or being born rich?

What about me? Trust, I know what it is, what it *means*, to be black – but not for nothing I got the whole Italian thing going on too. My neighbourhood's basically working-class, but my education's hoity-toity to the tenth power. It's a miracle I'm not in therapy with an identity crisis, but I know exactly who I am. The question is, why am I like this? I can cop to my shit – I know I'm not winning any Miss Congeniality awards; it's my way or the highway, and I don't take no mess. But how come? Is it a black thing? A Brooklyn thing? Or is culture irrelevant and who you are is a complete crapshoot?

Check out the 'frohawk – I'm wearing my culture clash on my head now. It's Epiphany's masterpiece. She conned A/B into jacking his dad's electric razor, then she carved it into my head.

223

Close-cropped on the sides – no actual scalp exposure – sloping up to the ridge. My mom and dad both shit a brick, but too bad on them: It's my hair. They're lucky I don't bleach it out and dye it green.

So I was loaded when I got it done – so what? I was *conscious;* it was a *decision.* I could tell Epiphany would do me right. Both those E Girls, I liked them from the get-go. No bullshit about them. All they wanna do is party with rock stars. Groupies. Now that's an anthropological ass-kick for you. I couldn't stop grilling them; not just about bands they banged but how they became groupies, what kind of network they have, what's the pecking order.

When I wasn't probing, I was busy observing how A/B and Wynn interacted with them. That hash was really opening my mind, all right. A/B? Textbook case of rock boy trying to act cool. But Wynn, it was weird. After Epiphany cut her hair – an edgy-shaggy modified mullet-that makes Wynn look even more like a model – it seemed like E2 had her flirt on full force. With me, E1 and E2 were just brassy-ballsy-big-sisterly, like the bad girls on the block who hung with your older brother and thought it would be fun to get you stoned. But with Wynn, E2 came on pure player – I heard her say Wynn's *wrists* were sexy, all right. It was hard to tell if Wynn was even aware of this.

Weird. But that's people for you. Weird all over. Even someone as on-point as Brian. Something's up with him. He stops into Broken Sound occasionally to see how it's going, discuss our agenda, and whatever. Face-time for us has always been rare, but there's this unspoken communication – a gesture, a smirk – that will happen between us even in a meeting. We still have it, but these days we hardly get a chance to indulge in it.

Look, I know it doesn't look good on paper, us as couple. We work together and that's textbook don't-go-there. And yeah, the age difference. But the age thing, working together – details like that shouldn't matter when two people connect like we do. Still, there's a chance he only likes me as a friend. Or maybe he's just blowing smoke up my ass to get the most out of me musically. Even worse, I could be walking around in a dazed, sappy stupor, and Brian could already have a girlfriend who he conveniently neglected to mention. No way in hell will I be the chick on the side!

I can't handle this, all right. I am not the type of person to sit around and chill. I need to know the score, one way or the other. So the time to be proactive is now! Only how? What should I say? Or do I say nothing and plant one on him – you know, like one kiss is worth a thousand words? Damn, this is so pathetic. Me, desperate for love advice. With no one, absolutely no one, I can talk to.

The Boy

Cowboy? Astronaut? President of the USA? Come on, it's got to be music for me. But stardom? Nah. Not that I mind the likes of the E Girls flinging themselves my way, but I'd be very happy with an under-the-radar career like Slushie's.

Famewise, we're the best thing Windows by Gina ever lucked into. *Wonder Bread* is their first-ever charting single, thanks to Kendall. Yet they're still a boutique band and always will be, while 6X is becoming a rock-and-roll Wal-Mart. Slushie can walk down the street unhassled; he can do his own music his way, produce people he likes and get paid for it and, the real key to his behind-the-scenes success, rule as a major jinglemeister. The ditties he writes help sell gum and cars and candy bars – they pay the mortgage on the Chelsea loft and the lease on that lavender Lexus.

Yeah, I'd be more than content to have that going on at his age. Something to shoot for, anyway. As to his relationship bliss – I got a whiff one night, when he had 6X to the loft for dinner – it's extremely doubtful I'll ever manage that. Slushie's married. His wife's *French*. Very pretty in that ooh-I-just-wake-up-like-zees sort of way. Her name's Sylvie. She runs one of those Chelsea art galleries, does photography – her stuff decorates their place – and even cooks: She whipped us up a cassoulet, which is like hot bean dip only fancier. And she and Slushie get along so well, like they're not trying at all.

Considering my batting average with the fair sex, I can only look at that in awe. Man, the way Kendall banged down the phone in Boston, I thought she was so pissed. The next day, go figure, she wasn't angry in the least (unless I misinterpreted the signals, what with a monster hangover making my head feel like an autistic kid's kick drum). She was worse than mad – she was over me. The way she sings *All Over Oliver* now, I can tell she'd love to substitute my name in the last verse, where the girl blows off her former crush in sassy female triumph. Used to be, when I hung out with her at Teen Towers, she'd be super-attentive. One time she even baked me cookies. Lately it's just . . . she's not cold, she's sweet – she just seems to have moved on. The other day I swung by on my way down from Penn Station, thinking we'd walk to Broken together; she let me in with a quick hello and trotted back to her laptop.

That's another twist. A month ago, I couldn't engage her in a friendly game of Snood; now she's got a brand new, top-of-the-line Mac with all the bells and whistles; she's even got Wi-Fi so she can go online anywhere, even at 35,000 feet. Still, it's not like she's turned into a complete geek. Kendall's Southern belle birthright, and all the man-tantalizing traps that come with it, is really starting to kick in. In fact, she's posing all these 'hypothetical' questions lately – out of nowhere she'll ask me: 'What do guys think of perfume?' or 'Do boys feel they have to pay for everything?' Stella would

say she's just playing me — trying to make me jealous.
Unfortunately it's kinda working . . .

The Voice

If it were not my God-given calling to entertain, I can think of no more noble and worthwhile mission than to be a wife and mother. I am confident that if my mom had not been forced to ascend in middle management due to my daddy's passing, she would have dedicated her life to our family. I bet I'd have a whole bunch of siblings, and Daddy would be so proud.

Of course, I do think it's possible to be a rock star and a wife and mother if your love is truly strong. Seeing as how I have met Mr Right, it's only natural for me to think about that. Gosh, I want to tell my mom about CountryBoy so bad. I think she'd approve of him – he's such a gentleman. He even asks me about my mom, and how many boys do you know who would be that considerate?

My secret is liable to sneak out on the plane to Atlanta. I'm already sorry that I told Wynn about CountryBoy (oh, I know his real name now: it's Jesse), but I had to tell *someone,* and Wynn's not one to go blabbing. Plus she gives good advice – although I cannot say I follow every word of it. For instance, she recommended that I not write back to CountryBoy; she said rock stars should keep fans in perspective. But CountryBoy is not just some regular old fan. He truly understands me.

Besides, she and Stella and A/B had no misgivings about carrying on with those girls in Boston. That really proved A/B unworthy of my love – and it made me feel even more strongly about Jesse. He makes me so happy even though we haven't met in person. Oh I did have my hopes up that he was a Georgia boy and could come to our Atlanta show. Well, he never did mention whereabouts he's from, but he admitted he has no car and couldn't get there. It's probably best for me to bond with my mom this weekend anyway – it's the first chance she's had to come to any of our away gigs.

And we're having such a great time. We had dinner – just us – at this real nice restaurant my mom had read about in a magazine. Now that I'm growing up, my mom and I are starting to be like friends. Of course I will always respect and obey her, but she is pretty young to be the mother of a teenager. She's also calming down some about everyone in Frog Level knowing my business. Malicious gossip – that's what worries her. But according to my grandmomma, people have only been saying the nicest things. Sure, I know *Dirty Boots* might be a bit rough for some folks, but heck, I don't think they listen to all the words; they just know I'm on MTV and Anderlee Bennett is with me and she's America's Sweetheart. Plus, *Wonder Bread* isn't a wicked song at all, so if people see me or hear me on that they can't say a bad thing.

In fact, I cannot think of one single negative word anyone in Frog Level could possibly say about me, my mom, my music, or anything.

The Body

Teaching kindergarten might be nice: molding innocent young minds. But what if personality is formed way earlier? Parents could easily screw you up in infancy. Still, things are at least simpler in kindergarten. Once puberty hits, forget it. I'd never want to be a psychologist, yet lately I feel like one.

Doctor-Love. Me, of all people. Too ironic! Of course I'm talking about Kendall's CountryBoy complex. It worries me. She's operating under the fantasy that he's actually her boyfriend – and while the things he says are sweet, I guess, and sensitive, his messages aren't precisely romantic, certainly not erotic; they're not love letters. Yet underneath the chaste charm the vibe I get is . . . *sinister,* like worms slithering around in all that e-mail mush. It's probably irrational anxiety, and even if it's not, he *is* CountryBoy – emphasis on country – and, from what I can tell, gathering the cash for a trip to New York would be one tall order for him. I should be glad Kendall's got something other than A/B to fixate on.

A band is much better off without romantic undercurrents – and the proof is in our recording sessions, which are going really well. There are still glitches, but we handle them now with newfound maturity. This Atlanta trip is another sign of our progress. Saturday afternoon we all hang at the hotel pool, and it's nice, mellow – you wouldn't be able to tell us from a group of friends on vacation, except when we get interrupted to sign a few autographs.

Come showtime, there's the typical stage fright we each have in our own way, but we're accustomed to each other's symptoms – and stay off each other's toes. And when we hit the stage, it's golden. Playing together in the studio almost every day makes us more confident musically, so we can be loose and truly enjoy performing. Even the new material we've added to the set feels high-energy, yet laid back. You know, fun.

After the gig it's all very PG. With Mrs Taylor chaperoning, the evilest thing we can imagine is going to this pancake house with an all-you-can-eat silver-dollar deal. It's really a scam – you pay more than you would for a single serving of silver dollars only to learn you can't possibly eat too many before feeling like silver dollar-sized slabs of lead have collected in your stomach. Hitting the pancake house must be *the* thing to do after a rock show in Atlanta; half the kids from the club are piled into booths. We get recognized but it's not a mob scene.

Coming home the next day, Kendall manipulates it so that her mom sits with Gaylord, and she and I are seat-mates, arrangements that'll let her safely chat with CountryBoy throughout the flight. Soon as we're airborne, she logs on to IM him, but since he's not online she sends him a long, convoluted e-mail. Next to her, I thumb through a tabloid (sorry, but I've so given up on Adrienne Rich) while providing her with vocabulary alternatives (adore? cherish? worship? really, really like?). Eventually she hits send and promptly nods off, the laptop open on her tray table. And she stays asleep, even when we hit some turbulence. The rough air rattles her computer, though. With a hiss it springs to life. The screen brightens. Lo and behold, Kendall has an IM.

OK, I know it's wrong. But I'm the one-and-only audience member to this soap opera and apparently the commercial's over. So I reach over. I touch a key. Up pops his message:

Darlin! I read your e-mail and you have a great idea. Wire me that money and I will get on the next plane to New York. Can't wait to be together!

The Boy

'We need to talk.' Cornering me in the kitchenette, Wynn digs gnawed-off nibs into my arm. 'A/B, this is serious.'

No shit. I release my precious bag of Kona-Colombian to give her my full attention, and she spills all: Kendall's e-mail paramour, his vague yet persistent weirdness quotient, and the nosy way Wynn learned of the twosome's plan to hook up in the flesh.

'We have to do something,' she hisses. 'What should we do?'

Wynn's in a panic and it's contagious. Sweet, innocent Kendall in the clutches of a possible psycho! Naturally, I scope out a loophole of denial. 'Are you sure about this?'

'Goddamn it, A/B,' she says. 'I read the IM with my own eyes. And the way she's acting, all fussy and flustered – she's so distracted she can't even sing *Hello Kitty*. She's going through with this, I can tell.'

It's true. Kendall's on her fourteenth take of *Hello Kitty Creeps Me Out*, and a Verdi aria it's not. But at least we can discuss the situation without fear of her busting in – until she nails the song, that is.

'OK, OK. We'll do something, we'll take action.' I'm trying

to keep it together, but fast-forward scenes of Kendall's imminent seduction (or worse) flip through my head like coming attractions on crystal meth.

'What, what?' Wynn wants to know. And she wants to know *now*.

'Shit, Wynn, I don't know. Let me think.' I think. 'I know!' I say.

She tightens her grip. I'm beginning to lose circulation.

'Let's tell Stella.'

Wynn lets go, emits a sigh crossed with a moan. 'That's your plan? Tell *Stella?*'

'Look, I know Kendall's not her favourite person but even if Stella were the devil incarnate, she's too protective of 6X to let anything happen to The Voice.' I tap my noggin and add, 'Right now I've got a hamster in a wheel up here. It's racing but going nowhere. Stella has got a mind like the proverbial steel trap. She'll know what to do.'

Wynn stares at me, unconvinced.

'Come on,' I urge her. 'It's the right thing. Definitely. We should tell Stella.'

'Tell Stella what?'

Debate over. Stella strides in, catching my last sentence. Wynn nearly leaps out of her skin, but I'm glad we've got no choice now. As we brief her, Stella ingests the info sans teeth-sucking sound effects. By the time we're done, she has a strategy.

'All right, if these star-crossed crackers are gonna hook up, it's gonna go down soon,' she says, hoisting herself onto the counter. 'He could be on the plane already. So we pretend like nothing and stake her out.'

Stella is Napoleon, Boris Spassky, and 007 rolled into one. Methodical. Steadfast. Three moves ahead. Wynn and I stand there as she goes on.

'We'll invite her to do stuff – not me, of course; even Kendall's smart enough to be suspicious if I start getting palsy-walsy. But . . . let me see . . . that chicks-in-rock documentary is playing at the Sunshine Cinemas. A/B, you tell her it's a must-see and ask her to go tonight. Wait, wait – she's over you; nothing would please her more than turning down a date with your sorry ass. Instead, say Brian wants her to see it. Then, Wynn, you tell her you've got a two-for-one special for a pedicure or some girly shit tomorrow. Remember, we're just waiting till she balks – then we know it's on.

'And we tail her. At a distance. Look, Kendall isn't exactly a walking Zagat's guide – how many places does she know? If she doesn't meet him at the Cup 'n' Saucer, she'll have him come to one of the places right on this block – maybe Donna's Donuts; she's always saying it's better than Krispy Kreme. Or that Starbucks across the street from the Teen Towers.'

At this point Stella addresses aloud what Wynn and I don't dare envision. 'No way she'd go to his hotel,' she says. 'We're talking Christian of the Year here . . .'

True, the Kendall we know wouldn't dream of meeting a guy alone in his hotel room. But is she still the Kendall we know?

The Body

It's amazing the way Stella takes charge of the situation. She marches back to the studio, and as we fall in behind A/B, all we see is Bertram, the lanky intern, fiddling with some wires. 'Hey, where's Kendall?' A/B asks.

'Dunno, mate.' Bertram keeps his head down and answers in the accent of someone who spent a semester in Sydney and came back with an affectation.

'You don't *know?*' asks A/B. 'What do you mean you don't *know?*'

Bertram looks up slowly. He's one of those slacker types whose expression never changes, a feat he probably had to practise. He's good at it. Gleeful, glum, annoyed – you really can't tell. 'I don't get paid to know,' he says dully. Returning to the electrical snake nest, he adds, 'I don't get paid, period.'

Slushie enters the big room, finishing up a cell phone call with his wife.

A/B gesticulates like an amateur mime-artist. Slushie regards him, quizzical, says, '*A beintot,*' and flips his phone shut. He takes in our stricken faces. 'Whoa, what's up?'

'Slushie, where's Kendall?' Stella asks calmly.

'Didn't she tell you? She has some kind of appointment . . .'

'She's *gone* . . . ?' A/B asks, not calmly.

'She's in the bathroom right now . . . but she says she's got to leave for a while,' Slushie informs us. 'How come you –'

At the sound of Kendall's footsteps, Stella makes a slashing motion across her throat: *Cut it!* 'So you think some atmospherics would sound good on that track, huh?' she says, convincingly coming off like we're discussing *My Real Dad Lives in Prague*, the next song we're set to record.

Slushie shrugs but plays along. 'Yeah, I thought I'd come up with some loops, you guys could take a listen, and we'll see what fits . . .'

A/B and I remain dumbstruck, furtively watching Kendall. She's changed into a frilly top and wears enough makeup to enter the Miss Teen Drag Queen contest.

'What do you think, Kendall?' Stella asks her, chill and smooth as a freeze-pop. Kendall doesn't hear, or is so wrapped up in her own thoughts she can't find the words to reply. 'Yo, girl, I'm talking to you,' Stella says with a snap.

'Oh, gosh, Stella. Yes, yes . . . that would be real nice,' she tells her handbag – she cannot meet anybody's eyes. 'So I'll be back soon, um, around four.'

Stella puts her hands on her hips, bugs her eyes. 'What?' she says with mock incredulity. 'You think you can just be out for three hours? You got any idea what studio time *costs?* You – you know what, forget it. Go on, whatever. *We'll* work with Slushie on the loops. Clearly, supah-stah, you've got priorities . . .'

'Stella!' Kendall's voice is petulant, but she quickly changes her tune. Stella's right: She *has* got priorities. 'Thanks, I'll, um,

238

oh, gosh – I need to . . . seeyoulater-bye.' Her last words gush out, and she's gone.

We wait about seven seconds, then spring. A/B races to the window in the reception area, clocks Kendall, runs back in. 'She's going towards Donna's!'

'Does someone want to tell me what's going on?' asks Slushie.

'Can't,' Stella says firmly. 'No time . . .'

As we tear out of Broken, we hear Slushie mumble, 'Guess I'll come up with some loops . . . or go buy toilet paper . . .'

The Boss

'Worst-case scenario.' Wynn slumps against the brick and whips off her shades. 'Oh God, you guys, I mean it,' she reports. 'It's bad.'

She doesn't have to say so. It's all over her face.

When we don't find Kendall in the donut shop, I realize that in her misty-pink mindset she'd want a more romantic setting for her rendezvous. So I send Wynn to check out the two competing bistros that face off against each other on opposing corners of Broome Street. Wynn will have no trouble sidling up to the bar; she'll look just like another Soho model, fashionably late to a shoot. We just have to risk that Kendall won't spot her spying. Now we're standing around near the service entrance of Comme du Buerre as Wynn lays it out for A/B and me.

'Apparently Kendall's gotten pretty sophisticated these last few months – she knew enough to make a reservation; I peek at the maître d's book and there's her name,' she says. 'I can't see where they've seated her, but I order a Coke and scope out the door. I see him saunter in – you'd have to be in a coma not to. He's one of *those* guys – part wolf, part puppy, part circus ringmaster . . . but mostly, I swear to God, Elvis.'

'As in Costello?' asks A/B.

Wynn appraises him like he's from outer space. 'As in *Presley*,' she says. 'And not fat, sequined jumpsuit Elvis either. *Hot* Elvis. Shoepolish pompadour. Dark denims with four-inch cuffs. White T-shirt with a bulge in the sleeve from a pack of smokes. Bleeding heart tattoo on a bicep that could crack walnuts.'

I know the type. 'Sounds like the guys who hang at Acme on Rockabilly Tuesdays. I went there for soul food with my parents once; it's like being in some fifties movie.'

'Exactly . . .' Wynn shivers in the sunlight – she is clearly spooked. 'So he's talking to the hostess while giving me the once-over at the end of the bar, and then he – he *winks* at me! With Tiffany-blue eyes you could see from a block away. I mean, he's bolder than a *New York Post* headline, just crass and obvious and crude . . . but he's got this charisma. I'm flattered in spite of myself. Of course, I refuse to hold his stare, so I watch my Coke like it might leap out of the glass.'

Wait a second. Wynn's actually impressed by a guy – and he's gaga for Kendall? Bananas! 'What makes you think he's CountryBoy?' I demand.

'When I hear the hostess giggle and assume he's giving her his full attention, I check him out again. Then I see what he has in his hand.' Wynn grimaces, flicks her fringe. 'Uch. A single red rose.'

She blinks hard, rips a cuticle with her teeth. 'As the hostess leads him to Kendall's table, I realize he's going to walk right past me. I keep staring at my soda. I smell cigarettes, the kind of men's cologne they must sell in gallon jugs. Then I don't know what comes over me but I'm compelled to look up. And I have to clutch the bar to steady myself. You guys, the thing is – he's old. Not old*er*, not twenty-something, I mean *old*. I swear, he's got to be at least *forty*.'

I take this in like a stiff drink, but instead of making me woozy I feel hyperaware. 'All right, this is worse than worst-case scenario,' I tell them. Clearly, we're out of our depths. I know what a freakin' paedophile is. I take out my cell to call Brian, get his secretary, tell her to drag him the hell out of his meeting *stat,* and she does it. I supply him with the edited highlights of what's going on, and he says we should head back to Broken and work on our music and not worry. He'll handle it.

And I'm relieved, really. I figure Mr Brian Wandweilder, big-shot Fifth Avenue attorney, will go down there and put the fear of the law into this pervert. And he does go down there. Only before he does, he makes a phone call of his own. After all, what does he really know about the tender hearts and fragile egos of teenage girls? He doesn't want to go down there alone.

The Voice

We are having dessert. Crème brûlée. Even though it's not chocolate, I love it, it's so elegant – the perfect final touch. Our lunch is lasting hours, and I don't want it to end. I decide to count this as my first date, because prom was a group – just a bunch of kids. This is what a real date should be. If it were nighttime, if there were candles, it would be perfect, but I don't dwell on that. It's still a French restaurant. The napkins are pink linen. The water is in wine glasses. And Jesse is more handsome than I would have let myself imagine.

When he first comes up to the table I'm taken aback. Because he's so good-looking, and also because he's older. I could tell from his e-mails he wasn't in high school anymore, but I figured he'd still be a teenager, maybe eighteen or nineteen. Well, he's quite a bit older than that – I can't tell his age for sure, and it's not polite to ask. But the way he says my name, his drawl so back-homey and sort of hushed like he can't believe he's actually with me – 'Kendall Taylor? Oh my, how pretty you are . . .' – I get a spongey, tingly feeling. He's just the sweetest thing. He brings me a single red rose, and when he sits, instead of handing it to me, bops the tip of my nose with it, then traces it down my cheek to my lips, which makes me smile.

Suddenly the age difference vanishes; it means nothing. We get along so well. And he makes me feel special, never being conceited and going about himself. Instead, he asks all about me – my school, my friends, and mostly the band and our record deal. He's just so interested in me. Of course I ask him questions back and, as it turns out, he's a singer too. Only not professional. He gets all shy and humble, saying he had a band once but they were just goofing around.

'I still love to warble a tune, though,' he says, and shows me a blinding flash of teeth, 'in the shower...' His smile turns wistful then. 'You know, Kendall, when I first saw you on MTV, I recollected one of my favourite songs.'

'Really?' And then I follow up. 'What song is that?'

Leaning forward, Jesse says, 'Come here.' I move toward him. He takes my hand, moves his mouth near my ear. His face is smooth, but I can count the hairs in his sideburns. His aftershave has this leafy, burnt aroma, and just the scent of his . . . Jesseness makes my head swim. Then he begins to sing, his voice a whisper melting on pillow: 'In dreams . . . I walk with you. In dreams . . . I talk to you. In dreams . . . You're mine . . . All of the time . . .'

The crème brûlée arrives – one serving, we're going to share – and we separate. He releases my hand and chuckles softly. 'Now that's Roy Orbison!' he says. 'You ever hear of him?'

'Um, nooo,' I say, reaching for a spoon. 'But that's such a beautiful song.'

'Well, you're young. Your mama, she ought to teach you

244

about Roy Orbison. He's one of the greats, but he's passed on now.'

'Oh,' I say, 'that's too bad.'

Jesse strokes his chin like he's thinking on something deeper and more important than dessert. Or maybe he's never had crème brûlée before, so I show him how to crack the glazed caramel crust with the rounded side of the spoon. The scent of sugar wafts up lightly between us. Then, just as I take a bite, I see him lift his gaze. The strangest look crosses his face — hard in a way, but also sort of satisfied — with those ice-blue eyes squinting and his mouth curving into a twist.

I turn to see what he's looking at just as I hear a voice say, 'Hello, Jesse.'

She doesn't look shocked or angry or hurt. Like him, she looks hard. There's a sort of satisfaction in her face too, like something she'd always dreaded had finally come.

This is a showdown.

'Well, hey there . . .' he says, smiling that twisted, satisfied smile.

I cannot close my mouth. The pale lump of pudding I've placed in it dribbles out and falls, slow-motion style, into my lap. The spoon slips from my hand, hits the blue tile floor with the peal of a tiny bell. The restaurant is fairly empty by now — the lunch crowd gone back to the shops and galleries of Soho — but Mr Wandweilder is here, frowning and leaning against an arch. He must have brought her here. Of course I recognize the woman behind my chair, staring Jesse down, but I can't figure out what she's doing here. And I don't want to. I keep turning from her to him, my mind burrowing like a frantic mole, but

245

the ground is crumbling, disintegrating, offering no haven, no place to hide . . .

Jesse stretches his arms out straight in front of him, cracks the knuckles of his right hand with his left, then repeats the gesture till all ten have made the sound of dry twigs crunching under a heavy boot. His smile grows bigger, more satisfied. 'What you been up to the last fifteen years, JoBeth?' he asks my mother.

That's when I notice my whole face is sticky and wet. I am crying, but the tears are absolutely silent. I understand, and understanding has a price: It steals my voice away.

The Boss

What a hot mess. And they say black people have drama. The band hasn't been in the studio for more than a week and no one will tell us the real deal – they're treating us like babies. It's so freakin' unfair. This is our lives here. Holed up in three different zip codes – A/B out on the Island, Wynn in Manhattan, and me in Brooklyn – all we can do is bitch and moan on the phone, trying to assemble snatches of facts like a jigsaw puzzle.

Here's what we've figured out:

All that garbage about Kendall's dad being a dead war hero? Ha! Her mom's been feeding her a steady diet of bullshit since the day she was born. Look up 'no-account redneck' in the dictionary and you'll see his picture. Jesse Taylor: part-time petty crook, part-time employee of a Columbia, South Carolina, web cafe (hence his Internet access), full-time asshole. There must have been a shotgun wedding out in the sticks some fifteen years ago to salvage the pride of Kendall's kinfolk. But Daddy didn't stick around, and the family was cool with that – good riddance to bad rubbish.

Except bad rubbish has a way of popping back up when it

smells a gravy train like a kid with a fat record contract. Jesse Taylor heard tell of his discarded daughter's ascension on the rock scene and went *cha-ching!* So he baited her in cyberspace and reeled her in like a largemouthed bass. So twisted – the poor kid believed he was her dream dude. Imagine jonesing for some guy . . . only to find out he's old enough to be your father . . . only to find out he is your father!

It's all too much for Kendall. After that fateful bite of crème brûlée in Comme du Buerre, she ran straight to her Teen Towers crib and hasn't set foot out of there since. At first, she wouldn't even let her mom in. Brian had called Mrs Taylor's office and had her meet him at the restaurant; neither one of them knew how freakydeaky the rendezvous really was, but he figured after he busted it up, her mom should be around to pick up the pieces. Now, under the circumstances, Mom's getting the silent treatment big-time.

If only it was restricted to her mother – but it's not. The Voice hasn't spoken a word – or sung a note – since the incident. Damn, if I learned my whole life and everything I believed in was a lie, I'd be howling like a banshee. Not Kendall. Is she pretending? Or is it bona fide hysterical muteness? Is her condition medical – or mystical? Sending her to a shrink is out of the question since her mom believes Freud was Satan's sidekick. Clearly Mrs Taylor is counting on prayer to heal her little girl's larynx. As to Kendall's for-lack-of-a-better-term 'father,' he must have found himself a shyster because he's sticking around to make a first-class pest of himself, demanding his rights.

Whether Kendall's faking or freaking, she's being equal

opportunity about it – she won't talk to any of us either. We've all tried e-mailing her, too, but not surprisingly she's lost her taste for chatting online. It's a full-on communication breakdown.

So where does that leave us? Roaming around like zombies in limbo. Nine songs in the can, seven more written and ready to record – but the sessions, the Chicago gig, our entire career has been put on hold. At least the powers that be aren't dragging their feet on damage control. Brian's wading through the legal muck. A final mix of *All Over Oliver* was 'leaked' to a downloading site – the label itself did the leaking, an effort to keep 6X in your face. And Universe wants the three of us to keep doing these video diaries so maybe there's some kind of backup plan if Kendall doesn't snap out of it.

Meanwhile, A/B's parents are all over his shit about college again. And Wynn's mom wants to take her to Switzerland for the rest of the summer – this 'spaspital' where Wynn can unwind from the whole ordeal, and Mrs Sherman can finally have something done about her infuriating frown lines. The only respite for me is my own parents had already bagged the family vacation (since I was supposed to be recording all summer), planning instead a second honeymoon in Niagara Falls. Thanks to small favours – and me assuring them I'm fine – they didn't cancel their trip, which means, starting tomorrow, I'll be left alone in brother JJ's care.

Normally, that would mean party. Yet even though I damn well deserve a chance to kick back and cut loose, I am just not feeling it. On the other hand, I refuse to sit around and mope – that's not Stella-style. So the first thing I'm gonna do is walk myself down to the handball courts and holler at my boy Tee. Yeah, it's been months, but he's still sweating me. And I feel . . . shit, I feel something shifting inside me, like I have reached my limit of career craziness and jumping through hoops and working my callused fingers to the bone – not to mention all the phonies and poseurs and freaks. Right now I just want to be with someone from the neighbourhood, someone I can talk to who I know just likes me for me. Someone *real*.

The Boy

Slowly but surely, my parents are driving me to the rubber room. They are not yelling; they are snuffling. They are not making demands; they are making helpful, hopeful suggestions. My father is taking me to play golf. Golf! Oy vey! If I say no, he practises his putt in the backyard, intermittently collapsing in a chaise lounge, wondering what he did wrong. My mother is buying me underwear. Constantly. Every day she goes out and by four P.M., I find my bed littered with boxers, briefs, threepacks of plain white tees, socks, socks, and more socks. It's as if I'd told her that I had indeed rethought my decision and come September will be packing for a university in a land before underwear.

I *have* to get off Long Island. It's not just my parents, it's . . . everything. The grass is too green, the girls too vacant, the cul-de-sacs too pristine. I take the railroad, but instead of heading to Penn, I change at Jamaica Station for the Brooklyn train, then study the subway map. I've concluded that a dose of Stella's tough love (OK, fine, tough *like*) will help preserve what remains of my sanity. I've never been to her house before, but I know the address and figure, hey, it's an adventure.

Yeah, Brooklyn. This is more like it. The riotous sunset over the Gowanus Canal. A greasy-garlicky rhapsody from the Chino-Latino joint on the corner. Kids toss a football in the middle of the street, screaming in singsongy Spanglish. Stocky men in wife-beaters hold court on their stoops, smoking, sipping from pints of tequila, assessing the passersby. Girls with earrings and asses like monuments rattle baby strollers absently while making assessments far more ruthless than those of the men; these girls are my age but I am not even worth a roll of their long-lashed, endless eyes. An ice-cream truck plays Christmas carols and hokey folk songs: *Joy to the World*, *On Top of Old Smokey*. Small, gutsy flower gardens fight for turf between trash cans and cast-off furniture.

Here it is, The Saunders' residence – a regal brown-stone in need of repair. I hit the buzzer, then lean on it. After a while, Stella's brother swings wide the door. He's wearing cutoffs and bunny slippers; in one hand he holds both a beer and a bagel.

'Hey, JJ, what's up?' I've met him before; he came to our showcase.

'I know you?' he says, nostrils flared like an animal testing my scent.

'Um, I'm A/B. I'm in Stella's band. You know, the guitarist.'

'Yeah?'

'Yeah.'

'So, what . . . you want something or something?'

It's difficult to believe that Stella is related to this troglodyte.

'Is Stella here?'

'Yeah, no, I dunno.' He bites a chunk off his bagel, washes it down with a swig. I don't see any actual chewing take place. 'You want I should call her for you?'

'Sure, that would be great.'

'Or you wanna just come in?' He punctuates the invitation with a belch. 'She's probably in her room. If she's here.' He shifts his eyes toward steps leading up. 'I live in the basement.'

Ah, I get it. Rather than make the effort to find his sister, he's willing to let someone he can't really recall meeting roam around his house. That sounds good to me.

'Sure, thanks. I'll just . . . I'll just . . . upstairs, right?'

'Yeah,' he says. 'Look, if you find her ask her if she's got ten bucks.'

'Oh, OK,' I say, moving past him. Halfway up the stairs, I hear him call.

'Hey . . . you.'

I turn around.

'*You* got ten bucks?'

I reach for my wallet, pull out a bill, and lean down to hand it over.

'You're all right,' JJ says and recedes down the hall.

As I travel up the stairs, some kind of distorted hip-hop/speed metal mélange, with lyrics bellowed in a language I can't identity, emanates from behind a door to my left. I bang on it. No answer. I turn the knob, and peer inside.

The room is gently aglow. Shadows pulsate on the posters lining the walls. Candles drip and flicker everywhere – on dressers, the bookcase, the top of the stereo, and all along a camp chest at the foot of the bed. Stella's bed. Upon which there are forms. There is movement. The forms are bodies. The movement is oh . . . my . . . God.

A flash of white across her shoulders – her yanked-up tank top. Below it, the long, smooth expanse of her bobs up and down. A syncopated, personal rhythm. It's Stella's own. She controls the tempo – this is how *she* likes it. The boy underneath her strokes her here, cups her there, reaches up for a handful of that wild hair. She dips or arches onto his hands, then slaps them away with a laugh.

'This is all about me, Tee,' she says, her voice like syrup – unlike I've ever heard it before. 'You're just along for the ride . . .'

That's exactly what I'm thinking! And knowing that I'm thinking what she's thinking is a shock, and I'm snapped out of slo-mo. I flinch – *shit!* – knocking something off the bureau by the bedroom door. *(Please don't let it be a candle . . .)*

'What the –?!' Stella sounds like Stella again.

'Wha . . .' echoes a slurry male voice.

Swivelling, she pulls the tank top over her boobs. She howls a string of curses followed by my name: 'A/B!!!'

As she jumps off the bed and hastily slings a sheet, sarong-style, around her waist, I raise my hand to my eyes. All I can say is 'Oops . . .'

The Voice (Within The Voice)

The world needs Kendall Taylor. Some might consider that a highfalutin thing to say about someone who's just the leader of a rock band, who's merely a pop culture phenomenon, who's only fifteen years old. But once in a blue moon a singer comes along who can do more than sing. She can reach and touch and move people. That's what Kendall Taylor does – but that's just one reason she's so important. With her values, her congeniality, and her empowering non-toothpick image, Kendall Taylor is already a role model too. And when young girls all over the country look up to a person, that person is obliged to put aside her own problems and be there for her public.

Not that this is easy. In fact, there's a part of Kendall Taylor that wants to act out. Slam doors. Throw things. Or even smoke. Or even drink. A part that wants to scream, 'Leave me alone!' And 'I am going to eat every last one of these donuts.' And 'No, I *won't* do that cameo role or appear in that Skechers ad or sign that licencing agreement or pose for that Kendall Taylor doll . . . *damn it!*' Or clam up, shut down, and not say anything at all.

Maybe stuff like endorsement deals and cameo roles sounds glamorous and fun. Well, they're not. They're sacrifices. Enormous sacrifices. Oh, they're not so bad when life is a petunia patch, but when a person is struggling, really struggling, with serious issues . . . it's so hard. When a person is feeling angry and bitter and betrayed and confused and embarrassed, it is almost impossible to be chipper and perky and nice.

But if a person is a star, bratty, selfish, bad-girl behaviour is not an option. Because a star has *responsibilities*. A star can't just fall apart like a junk-heap car up on blocks in some fool's front yard. A star can only comfort herself in the swaddling clothes of silence for so long until she remembers and accepts that it is her purpose in life – the reason she was put on this earth – to open her mouth and sing.

Something.

Anything.

Maybe *Amazing Grace*.

Maybe *Search and Destroy*.

That is the only option for Kendall Taylor. Sitting up in bed and singing her head off. Then marching her heinie back to Broken Sound and finishing her debut album, feeding all the torment of her family saga back into her music. That's what Kendall Taylor *has* to do – for her band and for all the people who depend on her and invested in her.

But mostly, like a true star, for her fans.

The Body

I've been musing lately. A lot. It's as if I feel so knowledgeable and sophisticated and aware – like I learned so much being in the band these last six months. Yet at the same time I am the most befuddled, ignorant doofus – I've been through so much but came out in a daze, going 'Huh? Wha? Where am I?' Basically, here's how it stacks up.

What I Don't Know:

- I don't know what makes people tick, what makes them do the things they do.
- I don't know why I do the things I do either.
- I have no idea what love is. Sometimes I feel like I'm out with a butterfly net, in a field full of love butterflies, but the holes in the net are too large, so whenever I think I've got love, it escapes. Love eludes me. But it doesn't fly away, exactly, it flies into my mouth – so it's inside me but I still don't know what it is.
- I don't know geometry. Somehow I managed to pass it but that is the miracle of the ages. Actually, not the miracle of the ages – it was sitting next to a boy so enthralled by

my chest he let me cheat off his paper. Go ahead. Ask me what an isosceles triangle is.
- I don't know what's wrong with me.

What I Do Know:
- I know how to play drums.
- I know how to write songs.
- I know that the more I play drums, and the more I write songs, the better I'll get at both.
- I know I am a poet. This is shocking to me – the shock has not worn off, it shocks me every time I think of myself as a poet – but in a good way.
- I know that evil exists. Evil is not just a concept to me any more. I've met it. I gave it my sweater. Then I puked all over it.
- I know that stressing out gets you nowhere. I know I will continue to stress out.
- I know that anything is possible . . . .

UNIVERSE RECORDS AND BRIAN WILSON WANDWEILDER, ESQ.
INVITE YOU TO A LISTENING PARTY CELEBRATING THE MOST
HIGHLY ANTICIPATED DEBUT OF THE YEAR!

6X
BLISS DE LA MESS

Friday, September 2ND
Otto's Hot Stack
67 Pearl Street
9 PM till . . . ?
Open bar all night

Special performance by 6X at midnight

Special guest DJ: Slushmaster Bongshaker

RSVP: Phoebe Stones (212) 555-1287

The Voice

This is so exciting – our record release party! This club, Otto's, it's the hottest place in New York right now, even though it's so downtown it's practically Brooklyn. It is a little sad to be shooting our last video diary here – but of course it's the perfect ending, since this is really just the beginning for us – for me.

The album turned out even better than I would have dared to dream. It sounds so good nobody will be able to tell the pressure I was under. My voice doesn't even hint at how hard it was for me. But it *was* hard. Lord only knows how I dragged myself out of bed, much less to the studio, what with all the monkey business that went on. The day of my . . . ordeal, I just shut down. Ran to Teen Towers and cried and prayed and cried some more. Bolted the door, too. My mom banged on it, begging me to let her in, until Mr Wandweilder led her away. He convinced her to let the TT staff look in on me for a day or two. He assured her that I would come around.

And I did. Pulled myself together. Allowed my mom inside. She took all the rest of her vacation time, bought an air mattress, and camped out in the apartment. Mostly I made like she wasn't there. All she wanted to do was talk, and I let her – but the only thing I had to say back was 'Uh-huh' and 'I see.' Every morning she'd fix me breakfast, which I wouldn't eat a bite of. I went to Donna's Donuts instead. I was so burning mad at her.

Now things are back to normal . . . on the surface, anyway. We speak, my mom and me; I mind her and all. Yet those wounds she inflicted – the lying, the hypocrisy – I don't know if they'll ever heal. Some people might say Jesse Taylor is a bad man; that he ran out on us and only came back to cash in on my success. But at least he didn't lie to me . . . not exactly, anyway. My mom on the other hand . . . there's a part of me that doesn't even want her here tonight, but I know that wouldn't look right. Appearances mean a lot when you're a star. That's hard to deal with too.

Anyway, there was just no way to keep such a scandal under wraps, so everybody found out – Mr Wandweilder, my bandmates, even the intern at Broken and the counter girl at Donna's. The way all of them were tippy-toeing around – Stella too!

Then I'd go in the booth and put on the headphones. I'd hear our music pouring over me and through me like a cleansing rain. And my voice just lifted out of me. My darkest despair and the brightest, most glorious parts of my soul converged. At times it would literally make me tremble. That is the power and beauty of being blessed with a voice like mine.

The whole experience – I liken it to certain Bible stories. Like Jonah in the whale. Or Job with all his trials and tribulations. Or even like Jesus Christ the Lord himself. After a long day and night in the recording studio, I would lie down to think on these tales, and take comfort in knowing that I was akin to a super Bible hero myself. I weathered the storm. I arrived triumphant. And now . . .

Whoooo-hooooo! How's that for a rebel yell?

Tonight is *my* night. It's time to party! I can do whatever I please. Tonight Kendall Taylor will bust loose like never before . . .

The Boy

Why they call this a listening party is a mystery to me. Everyone's so busy yammering away – who can hear? I wish everyone would shut up and listen to the music, but I guess that would be a pretty dull party. Well, no worries – they'll be giving out goody bags at the end with our CD in them. But allow me to inform you in advance: Our record rocks!

Yeah, I care about reviews and everything and I hope the critics like it, but the most important thing is that I'm happy with it. And I am. I can't even be sarcastic or shrug it off with très hip alt-rock attitude. I LOVE *BLISS DE LA MESS!*

Don't take this the wrong way, but I feel like I gave birth to this record. I mean, I spent almost as much time mixing the damn thing as recording it – not that I actually mixed it myself, but I was at every session, while the girls were off doing girl things. After all, they are girls . . .

Boy, are they girls. Which is a beautiful thing. Being in 6X is like an AP class in all things female – oh, the insights I have gleaned! But the more you learn, the less you know. Just when you think you've got the chick psyche down, they flip you. Take sex, for instance. I would have sworn all girls follow a traditional love-and-romance rule book à la Kendall, but then along comes Stella. Now there's a girl with a healthy attitude. That time I caught her in flagrante delicto – which is Latin for getting laid – she wasn't even embarrassed. Pissed, yeah, sure, understandably so. Soon as she calmed down, though, she was just like, 'Excuse me, can't you see I'm busy?'

Unquestionably, I was more mortified than she was, and she dealt with that too. 'Look, why don't you go downstairs, take a beer from the fridge, and me and Tee'll come down in a few.' Just perfectly rational and chill. And half an hour later we're all hanging out, Tee turning me on to the Dominican speed-metal-emo-hip-hop hybrid he's into, even promising to make me a mixtape. Pretty decent guy, that Tee. Nice of him to, you know, not murder me for my third-party coitus interuptus. Cool as he is, though, I'm glad he's not Stella's date tonight – they've got more of a friends-with-benefits thing going on. Don't ask me why this pleases me – I have no clue.

That's why it's nice to have something I'm unequivocal about. To wit, our record. Bottom line, it's awesome! But hey, don't take my word for it! Here comes our lovely and talented lead singer, Miss Kendall Taylor. Let's hear what she has to say.

'A/B! A/B! Isn't thish the besht party ever?'

'Whoa, Kendall, don't fall down. You OK . . . ?'

'OK? Yesh, A/B, I am. I am fantaaaashtic.'

'So here we are, filming the final entries of our video diaries. How'd you like to give all our fans out there your unbiased opinion of *Bliss de la Mess?*'

'Oh shweet Jesush! Oh gosh! It rocksh! Everybody should rush right out and buy it so we can become billionairesh! No, no, no, sheriously. Making thish album was so fulflilling. Even though there were some tough thimesh, right, A/B? But we did it! We *did* it! And I love you all. The fansh, everyone at Universh, Mishter Weildwander, Shtella, Wynn . . . and you, A/B. Mosht eshpecially I . . . love . . . you!'

'Wow, Kendall, you really seem to be having a blast tonight. Whoops, there you go again. It's OK, I got you! You and those wacky high heels! Anyway –'

'Oh loooook! It's Reid-Vinshent Mitchell. Gosh, I jusht love him. Heyyy! Reeeeid-Vinshent!'

Well, there she goes, folks, in true rock star form. Hey, I could be wrong, but it looks to me like Miss Kendall Taylor has discovered champagne.

The Boss

I am having the best time! I was kinda cranky all day, wondering if Brian was gonna bring a date. That probably would have pissed me off big-time, watching him make his entrance with some dumb model. But as far as I can see, he is flying solo and that is a load off. But check it out: I might actually be over Brian anyway. Yeah, he is awesome and we're still completely simpatico, but he is older and the whole thing with Kendall and CountryBoy kinda put a bad taste in my mouth about that. Like, it is a little gross. Like, I don't wanna be changing his incontinence pads down the line, all right.

Ha-ha. Just kidding. I'm not completely counting him out because hey, look at my parents. Back in the day, her being white and him being black was a big deal. So all I'm saying is life presents challenges but love can conquer them. All I'm saying is, 'Who knows?'

It's more that, right now, settling down is not on my agenda. *Bliss de la Mess* comes out this Tuesday, and we shipped platinum, which means a million 6X albums are going into stores. That's very unusual for a debut. Once the record drops, of course, we're gonna go on the road – and I can't wait! Thing is, that's gotta be tough on a relationship; you don't want to be worrying if your boyfriend is creeping when you're hitting the stage in Buttzit, Nebraska. Plus, who knows who I'll hook up with when we're out? Touring is like this whole smorgasbord of hot guys. We could go out with the Blokes or Ayn Rand or maybe we'll open for Churnsway – now Lucien Vickers, that boy could get it. Besides, you can't predict – sometimes the right person, the guy you'll stay crazy in love with forever, can come at you completely out of nowhere . . . or be right under your nose . . .

The Body

The mess is forgotten and all that's left is the bliss. For about an hour anyway . . .

I'm not a huge party person but tonight even I got caught up in the vibe. All the usual suspects are in attendance: Windows by Gina, Tiger Pimp, all those guys. But not just music people. Crimson Snow and Jake Pfstaad actually came. And Malinka Kolakova, the Russian tennis ace – she just won Wimbledon? Her people got my people to introduce us, and she's so beautiful and nice and we've been talking, although her English is not the best . . . In fact, it's hilarious.

Then *All Over Oliver* comes on – yes, it's set to be the first official single from the album – and Stella hauls me onto the floor and we start dancing. Everyone follows – I swear it's like the entire hipster population of New York City is getting down to our song. And when the chorus kicks in? They all know the words already. Not that it's Sylvia Plath or anything, but hearing the whole club scream, *'Now I'm all over Oliver, oh yeah!'* it's . . . I'm sorry, but it's incredible.

At first I had my doubts. I worried people would see a young band that got real hot real fast and think we're a gimmick or a one-hit wonder. Then I was like: *Who cares what they think? I'm in 6X – and I know better. We'll be together forever.* And the best part is, with everyone digging on us, it's still just Stella and me dancing together.

Then Stella scrunches the crown of her 'hawk. 'Damn, Wynn, are we the shit or what?!' she says.

I'm about to throw my arms around her – I'm so emotional, I figure a hug can say what words cannot. Only, classic Stella, she switches back to business mode.

'Come on,' she says. 'Time to get serious – we're going on soon.'

So we start scoping the place for A/B – which ought to be easy, since he's got on this ridiculous silver pimp jacket we found at a thrift store. We see him by the bar with Gaylord and Brian. Our boys. They seem to be scoping for us too, since we need to go backstage, tune up, run a few licks. For the first time I have zero stage fright. I think, *Playing tonight will be a prime example of what Kendall would call 'preaching to the choir.'*

That's when this weird, almost psychic sensation comes over me. I try dismissing it, telling myself I'm crazy, that nothing's wrong. But as I follow Stella to the bar, this nagging little uh-oh grows.

'So it's gotta be close to showtime, no?' Stella says to the guys.

Brian checks his watch. 'Pretty much,' he says. 'Anyone see Kendall?'

The mention of Kendall's name makes me feel nauseous. The uh-oh feeling goes *nyah-nyah*. But I don't want to be Debbie Downer; I keep my mouth shut.

'Just find Mrs Taylor and look in the opposite direction,' Gaylord suggests with a smirk.

'Hey, none of that.' Brian tries to conceal a smirk of his own. 'JoBeth Taylor hasn't exactly had an easy time with Kendall lately.'

That's when A/B thumps his forehead with the heel of his palm. 'Shit!' he says. 'I can't believe I didn't tell you – I spaced that we're even playing tonight . . .'

'Tell us what?' Brian asks casually, purposefully keeping alarm from his voice. But I meet his eyes, and for one flash, we connect. He's caught my uh-oh feeling.

'Um, don't shoot the belated messenger but Kendall is rather plastered.'

Nobody believes this – everyone starts in at once: Kendall? Drunk? No way! Never happen!

'I'm telling you, I saw her twenty minutes ago,' A/B insists. 'And she was *low-ded.*'

'Where?' Brian asks as calmly as he's capable.

'Hmm, near the buffet . . . no, no, no.' A/B sweats his memory. He's a bit buzzed himself. 'Oh yeah, it was in the alcove where the cameras are set up. We talked for a minute and then she tottered off. After that actor guy, the one with the three first names – the *Steal That Pony* dude.'

Brian's still feigning this it's-all-good attitude. 'Well, we should look for her,' he sighs. 'There's time to pump her full of H_2O and coffee before you guys have to go on.'

Stella seizes the opportunity. 'That stupid little chickenhead!' she explodes. 'Leave it to Kendall to wreck our party, sabotage our show. I'm telling you guys, I'm about done with that one.'

'Stella, please,' Brian says. By now we all see he's serious. 'Let's just find her, OK?'

Just as we're ready to spring into action, Gaylord spots a sore thumb in lavender blouse, navy business suit, and sensible pumps coming at us, 'Mrs Mayberry at three o'clock, approaching fast,' he warns.

Brian checks his watch again, mutters. The plan is to fan out, scour every inch of Otto's. There's a chill out (read: make-out) zone upstairs – maybe Kendall and R-VM are getting busy. Or she could be in the bathroom, worshipping the porcelain god. Or ha-ha, we're punked – she might be backstage already, warming up her voice, waiting for us.

Stella and A/B head upstairs. Gaylord aims for backstage while Brian will play interference with Mrs Taylor. I volunteer for bathroom duty. But I know I won't find Kendall there. My suspicions have settled into smug fact. We're just going through the motions, exhausting every commonsense possibility because we're supposed to hit the stage in half an hour, and we don't want to accept what I already know. This is a snipe hunt – a futile pursuit. After all, when you're in a band with someone for a while, and you go through the kind of stuff 6X has, you don't simply *know* them, you *are* them – a part of you is them, and a part of them is you. You don't have to predict what they'll do. You just know. Like I know:

Kendall Taylor has left the building . . .

Kendall Taylor is not in the house . . .

Kendall Taylor is gone . . .

6X is who...?

Kendall Taylor
Voice

A/B Farrelberg
Guitars, Keyboards, Whatever

Wynn Morgan
Drums, Voice

Stella Angenue Simone Saunders
Bass

Tracks:

1) Dirty Boots
2) All Over Oliver
3) Bliss de la Mess
4) Put This in Your Purse (Ashley)
5) You're All I've Got Tonight†
6) My Real Dad Lives in Prague
7) (I Am Not a) Lingerie Model
8) The Waiting˜
9) Hello Kitty Creeps Me Out
10) Teenage FBI^

Produced by Alan Slushinger. Mixed by Lydia Vance. Recorded and mixed at Broken Sound, NYC. A&R: Preston Shenck, Management: Gaylord Kramer, Straight Man Management. Photography: Jason 'Part III' Stutts. Web design: Nathan DaWeen

Publishing: All songs (except *, †, ˜, ^), Lyrics by Wynn Morgan, Music by Taylor, Farrelberg, Morgan, Saunders (HotShit Music/BMI); * by Sonic Youth; † by Ric Ocasek; ˜ by Tom Petty; ^ by Robert Pollard

A lotta love and thanks to . . .

Jesus Christ, JoBeth Taylor, Arness and Lilly Clark, Brian Wandweilder, and all the amazing fans! – **KENDALL**

Lynda and Martin Farrelberg, Brian Wandweilder, Gaylord Kramer, Alan Slushinger, Martin Guitars, Dan Electro Guitars, and all those about to rock, who are rocking now, and who have rocked in the past, from AC/DC to ZZ Topp! – **A/B**

Cynthia and Randall Sherman, Brian Wandweilder, Gaylord Kramer, Travis Brown, and every single nice person and animal on the planet – **WYNN**

Victoria and Derek Saunders, John Joseph Cantaluccl, Brian 'The Man' Wandweilder, Gaylord Kramer, Charisse 'Boom Boom' Thomas, the Ramones, and you, yeah, you! – **STELLA**